Taboo Frequency

Smoke, Inc.

Gem Sivad

TABOO FREQUENCY
Smoke, Inc.
By Gem Sivad

Taboo Frequency

Smoke, Inc.

When ultimate impulse collides with maximum control...

It's all about taking charge. Luke Danvers has his future planned to the nth degree—until he steps on an IED in Afghanistan. Bitter, angry, and emotionally adrift, he returns to the States, ready to spend the rest of his life pissed off at the world.

Kiley Endicott has never been a poster child for moderation. Married and widowed young, she's raising twins on her own. Since impulse has always ruled her life, it's not easy being a sedate parent under the critically watchful eye of her family.

A Friday night lapse in sanity leads Kiley to a hookup with Luke Danvers. Even in the cab of a truck, he's an awesome lover. She wants more. But she's got to be circumspect; nobody can know.

Luke hasn't had fun in—forever. But he can't stop grinning after he meets Kiley Endicott. It's more than her being a totally uninhibited lover, but God knows he can't get enough of that either. She makes him laugh.

She says nobody can know. Okay, he's trained in stealth. He sets up a call system, a taboo frequency, guaranteeing her twenty-four-hour access in every way. But he's not just waiting for their secret meets. He's planning a siege.

Acknowledgements

Much appreciation to editor Mary Harris and V.N. Johnson for pointing out plot problems and helping me develop Kiley and Luke's story.

As usual, Cover Designer Kristian Norris interpreted my inarticulate longings and produced *Taboo Frequency*'s beautiful cover.

And last, but certainly not least, thank you, family. Without you, the stories end.

Prologue

STARKLY ALONE, THOUGH he stood among a cluster of homeless men huddled under the Angel House sign, Luke Danvers stared at the ground, waiting for the shelter to open. The mild January weather Austin had been enjoying had turned cold earlier in the day, and a lot of people were looking for a space inside for the night.

After he'd checked out of the VA outpatient clinic, he remembered withdrawing cash from an ATM, then visiting a blur of bars, none of which he could name.

His wallet and phone were missing along with the money. Pain throbbed in his skull. He touched the back of his head and discovered dried blood covering a sizeable lump.

He figured he'd run out of money and drinking buddies about the same time. Maybe one of them had decided to drink alone on Luke's dime. He probably needed to report things, but he didn't care enough about any of it to make the motions.

His stomach growled, surprising him. It had been awhile since he'd felt hungry. *Booze must be wearing off.* He fumbled for the flask in his jacket, hand coming away empty.

Dammit. Where the hell is... Losing his liquor bothered him a lot more than losing his wallet. He pondered that, knowing it was a significant marker on his slide into hell.

I should drink to that. The day I didn't give a shit about anything anymore. While he contemplated the disintegration of his character, a fancy Dodge Challenger roared up to the shelter.

A moment before, Luke had severed all ties to giving a damn about anything. But when a familiar figure stepped from the car, he shuddered.

Shit. That's Micah Wolfe. Can't let him see me like this. Shame cut through the former master sergeant and he turned away so fast he swayed, almost going down.

Mother of God don't let me fall now. Food and shelter forgotten, Luke fled. No way could the friend he'd fought shoulder to shoulder with in combat see the derelict Luke had become.

Chapter One

*D*AMMIT. LUKE'S FROWN changed to a full scowl as he paused at the exit to pull on his jacket. When he'd walked into the VA Hospital, the April sky had been overcast, threatening bad weather. During his visit, the gloom had segued into icy rain, making it a wet, slippery night in Pittsburgh.

"Would you like some company, Master Sergeant Danvers?"

The soft voice asking the question didn't startle him. Melissa's perfume had announced her long before she arrived. After his prothesis adjustment, Luke had stopped to visit Donnie Blanco.

The other soldier lay hooked to machines, his mind gone, and his body screwed up beyond repair. Before Luke had split with his ex, they'd partied with Donnie and his wife, Melissa. A lot had changed since then.

During Luke's short time in the room where Melissa kept her silent vigil, she'd watched him with hungry eyes, then followed him down the hall when he left.

Whether she was offering Luke a pity fuck, or hoping for a shoulder to cry on, neither held any appeal. Not turning to look, he used his key fob to remote start his truck and kept staring outside.

"Nope, I'm good." He finished shrugging into his coat before meeting her gaze.

Her blush made her skin glow. At the same time, he inhaled her flowery female scent and his groin tightened, suggesting he might have been too quick in dismissing her offer.

"Take care, Mel." Luke left the building before he could change his mind. Having no desire to fall on his ass and break his good leg, he made slow work of crossing the icy parking lot to his truck.

Once inside, he sat in the cab with the engine idling, not ready yet to start the long drive to the empty house he now called home. When he'd bought the buildings and acreage, he'd had a plan. Same with the truck.

Yeah, right. You had a plan. His leg ached and he reached down to rub the phantom limb, touching the artificial replacement instead. It filled out the leg of his jeans and he didn't limp much anymore. That didn't stop a surge of rage from clawing at his throat.

"Shit." He sat a while longer, reeling in his anger and tucking it away in the steel locker of his resolve. But he wasn't ready to carry all that resolve home to an empty house. Besides, he had an invitation of sorts to a party.

He'd found a missed call and message on his phone, right before he'd gone into the VA hospital.

"Hey, Luke. Stop by if you have time, Friday. Micah will be at my place."

If I have time. He snorted in disgust. All he had was time.

He'd seen Micah in Austin, and not wanting to shame himself in front of a friend, he'd moved away from Texas.

Luke hadn't joined the local social club upon taking possession of his farmhouse. But, having served with Doug Blake in Afghanistan, he'd made a courtesy call when he moved close enough to claim him as a neighbor.

Since then, Luke considered his life improved. The land he owned wasn't much. And his social skills were still a work in progress.

Though he still wasn't the man he needed to be, he was better now than the drunk he'd been turning into in Austin. Most of the time he still walked around feeling hollow inside. Like he wasn't quite real.

Recently, he'd been thinking about getting cozy again with a bottle of Jack. He licked his lips, almost tasting it. He could turn right and be in a bar in five minutes.

Nope. Not tonight. Maybe it was time he said hello to a different old friend. Luke put his F-150 in gear and drove out of the now slick parking lot. Turning toward I-79 South, he headed out of Pittsburg, toward Waynesburg and Blake's house in the country.

Even if his GPS locator had failed, he couldn't have missed it. A huge basket spilling colored eggs decorated the lawn and a giant rabbit held a sign that said *Blake's Place.*

Music, a blinking neon light, and a pointing arrow all indicated he'd find the party out back.

That's dance music. Shit. He'd been planning on sports, talk, and TV. He slowed the truck to a crawl.

I should go on home.

The front door swung open and bodies spilled outside. A familiar shit-eating grin swung Luke's way and got bigger when he locked gazes with its owner.

"'Bout time you got here, Danvers," Micah Wolfe drawled. "Park it and come out back."

Nobody seemed to care that the earlier rain had drenched things. Or that bonfires were for fall.

Blankets covered the improvised seats, ringing the crackling firepit. For the next half hour or so, Luke sat on a bale of straw and watched Micah repeatedly check his watch as he told stories about his wife, Madison.

It was clear he couldn't wait to get back to her. The conversation ended when it was time for him to catch his plane to Austin.

"You're lookin' real good, Luke. Sorry I've got to cut this short. Stay in touch."

After Micah left, Luke kept his seat on the bale of straw, his hat brim pulled low enough to shield his eyes, hiding his interest from the others as he studied the woman sitting across the fire.

He knew he knew her, but for the life of him, he couldn't remember how. She looked familiar but wasn't one of the local women he'd encountered. Nor did she seem like someone he'd met during a foray at the nearby VA hospital.

Her expression remained guarded, though she smiled and did the female chitchat thing with the other women.

She hadn't responded when one of Doug's buddies sat next to her and attempted conversation. When she hadn't appeared interested in a hookup, the guy moved on.

Luke's gaze wandered past her and paused on Doug's wife. Then he shifted back to the mystery woman.

"Marcie, I didn't know you had a sister," he called across the fire.

"Most people don't think they look anything alike. How did you know?" Doug slung a possessive arm around his wife's shoulders as though Luke might be planning to snatch her away.

"The shape of the nose and eyes are the same," Luke answered, ignoring Doug's paranoia.

I'd probably be a possessive sonofabitch if she was mine, too. Luke settled his gaze on Doug's sister-in-law.

"She's my twin, not just my sister," Marcie admitted and grinned.

"*She* is sitting right here and *she* is not deaf and dumb." Marcie's sister stood, circled the fire, and held out her hand. "I'm Kiley Endicott, nice to meet you… again."

"Hard to believe you're twins," he answered, taking her hand and liking the way it fit in his big paw.

He felt like maybe he'd missed part of the conversation when she continued standing above him so that he had to tilt his head to meet her gaze. Then he realized he hadn't released her hand.

"Sorry," he mumbled, dropping it. "I'm Luke Danvers, nice to meet you since I don't recall being formally introduced before. There's room on the blanket if you want to share."

"Do you *mind* if I sit next to you?" Her question surprised him.

Mind? Hell no. He scooted sideways, making room before she changed her mind.

She sat, not touching, but close enough for him to feel her body heat. He rubbed his jaw, wishing he'd taken time to trim his beard before his VA visit today. Parts of him began to thaw and his brain returned to the certainty that he'd met her before.

He'd never been accused of being couth, so he didn't pretend. He turned, focusing all his attention on her face. Not that he hadn't already catalogued her lithe build, long legs, perfect ass, and beneath her pink sweatshirt, nicely rounded breasts.

She was a damn fine-looking lady. More than likely a soccer mom. Since Luke hadn't seen her attached to a soccer dad, he enjoyed the view. She'd pushed a pair of sunglasses up on her head and they served as a headband, holding back a swath of thick, curling, golden brown hair.

Hair he'd like to run his hands through. Arched brows, high cheekbones, straight nose with a sprinkle of freckles, beautiful mouth…

Luke's gaze stalled on the full, lower, bitable lip. He'd never met this woman before, and yet he had. He tipped his hat back, squinting as he studied her closer.

"Still don't remember me, huh?" She flashed him that sly grin that looked so familiar, teasing his memory until it hit him.

"Well, I'll be damned. You're Evan Endicott's blue-haired girl." And then all the links connected, and a flush crawled up his neck. The first and *only* time he'd met

Endicott's woman, Luke had been knee-deep in a first-class fuck-up with his former wife.

His re-up date had arrived, and he'd decided to stay stateside and settle down. Unfortunately, his *un-enlistment* party was going strong before he'd bothered telling Shelley what they were celebrating. With whiskey in hand, he'd held her close and toasted the occasion.

"Here's to two point five kids, a beautiful wife, a spotted dog, and a little patch of ground."

She'd smiled up at him serenely. She'd heard that toast so many times, he'd been sure that she didn't believe it and proud that this time he had something concrete to throw in with the words.

"I signed the papers on that property I told you about. Now, all we need is a dog and we can start on the kids."

Seven years later, Luke still gritted his teeth, the memory making him feel like a fool all over again. Shelley had freaked, not caring at all if she was overheard.

The gist of her message had been plain enough. Him being gone on missions and her being left behind with his monthly allotment had suited her single lifestyle fine. Having a real marriage didn't fit into the scheme of things.

"We don't even know each other any longer. I don't want children or a rundown farm in the middle of nowhere. We have nothing in common but a last name and that's easy enough to fix." She'd meant it, too.

Endicott and wife had entered during Shelley's tirade. The kid hadn't seen combat duty, and innocence still marked his expression. His wife had appeared even younger.

Kiley Endicott had stood in the room, wearing assorted piercings and neon blue hair brushed up in a crazy Mohawk style. Balancing a toddler on each hip, she'd looked like someone's twelve-year-old babysitter.

But then she'd flashed him that sly grin, like she'd seen it all before. Even through Shelley's rant, he'd registered the cynical smile.

It hadn't taken Endicott long to drop off the keg he'd brought with him and leave with his family. Luke had felt ancient gazing after the young couple.

Shelley hadn't lingered either, but the booze had been delivered, so Luke had gone ahead with the party. He didn't remember much of it later because he'd mixed his shock with Jack Daniels. But he remembered Endicott's wife.

He'd sobered up the next day and split the bank account with Shelley. He'd let her go without a fuss and expedited the paper work so she could get a quick divorce.

Then he'd put the fiasco of his marriage behind him and signed up for another tour in Afghanistan.

Might have been better to have skipped that last part. When he'd been in first tour battles, the enemy had been using mostly mortar fire and grenades.

By the second tour, they'd come up with something everyone called IEDs—***improvised explosive devices.*** The incendiaries were nothing more than homemade booby traps.

Whatever you called them, the other side had figured out that IEDs were easy, cheap, and carried a hell of a kick, both physically and mentally. There wasn't a man in his unit who hadn't been scared shitless every step of the way.

Luke grimaced, flexing ghost muscles that ached in his nonexistent lower leg. He'd had enough knee left for the surgeons to attach a prosthesis. Endicott hadn't been so lucky when he stepped wrong.

Luke stared at the kid's wife, now a sedate widow wearing light brown curls and no face jewelry.

"If it means anything, after all this time," he drawled, looking at the new version of Endicott's blue-haired girl. "My apologies for the public brawl."

✧   ✧   ✧

"APOLOGY ACCEPTED," KILEY answered. The fake smile she'd worn earlier for the sake of Marcie's party warmed a bit as she gazed at Luke Danvers. "I remember you as well."

"Well damn. That's not good," Luke groaned.

Whoa. What's this about? Kiley's insides clenched, responding to the gravelly texture and low timber of his voice.

"I'm executing an extraction plan at the moment," she confided, her pulse quickening as her words emerged in husky tones she barely recognized.

"Do tell," he drawled, making other parts of her quicken again.

"I arrived late to the party and plan to leave early. My strategy—drift around the campfire, reach the shadows, and wait until eyes are elsewhere—then duck out for the night."

"So you're waiting for someone to shoot off a rocket or something?"

"Maybe. Getting away from Marcie takes mad stealth

skills." She knew she was babbling but couldn't shut herself up.

Her sister, who worried about Kiley's social life, or lack thereof, beamed at her from across the bonfire. Even from that distance, she could see the speculative gleam in Marcie's eyes.

She'd targeted Luke Danvers as a likely exit point since he didn't seem interested in company. She'd headed for him, figuring that she'd say hello and then beat a fast retreat.

"I've gotta tell you, I like the new look." He smirked at her, reminding her that he'd seen her in her blue phase.

"I quit dyeing it weird colors when the twins were babies." Kiley touched her hair self-consciously. Belatedly, she remembered the last time she'd seen him: he'd been arguing with his wife about leaving the military to take up farming.

"Did you get your patch of ground?" she asked, discreetly checking easy exits from the firepit.

"Sure did," he answered.

To stay or not to stay? He was drinking bottled water, not beer, so she wouldn't have any trouble managing a drunk. She emptied her beer on the ground behind the straw and got comfortable next to him.

"Not much of a drinker, huh?" Luke drawled. "You looked like a hell-raiser when you were younger."

"I could say the same about you. As I recall, you were drunk, unruly, and arguing with your wife the last time I saw you."

"Ex-wife now." He slid that information in as if it mattered. "Obviously, things changed for both of us," he said gruffly.

"Yes," Kiley agreed. She felt out of breath, as if she'd been sparring with swords instead of words. Heat pooled in her belly and her nipples were peaks of sensitivity poking dents in her sweatshirt.

"I'm a farmer now."

God, I'm pitiful. I might jump on this poor man if he says much more. Nevertheless, she kept the conversation going.

"What do you raise on your farm?" She waited for him to answer, ready to endure tales of pigs, or corn, or steers to hear more of the rumbling tones coming from him.

He seemed at a loss for words, as if unsure what crop or herd he tended on his land.

✧   ✧   ✧

LUKE STALLED IN his pickup line, which wasn't a line, more like a pathetic attempt to keep her interest.

"Evergreens," he improvised. "I grow Christmas trees."

He'd bought his place by doing a web search for property available in rural areas around Pittsburgh.

"Your brother-in-law talked me into this area."

"You mean Doug?"

"Yep. He was my platoon leader, First Lieutenant Doug Blake."

Doug had offered suggestions, telling him about the place where his wife's family lived. Luke had closed the deal based on a realtor's picture and never visited his purchase until he'd been wounded in Afghanistan and deployed home.

He'd hung onto the land as an act of defiance when

Shelley dumped him, but it had become an anchor when he was in the hospital.

While he'd been fitted for his fake leg, he'd had a place to call home when he got out and plenty of time to make plans about what he'd do once he moved in.

But after his hospital release last December, he'd stayed drunk in Austin for a while. It wasn't until he'd caught sight of Micah Wolfe, he'd remembered the land. Then he'd tucked tail and headed north.

Since taking possession of his place, he hadn't done much more than fix the barn and patch the roof of the house. He'd spent most of the spring learning to navigate the uneven terrain using his new leg. As far as running a working farm, well…

He knew as soon as she sat next to him that he wanted to have sex with her. She smelled good, getting his cock's attention immediately.

After they'd talked about not much of anything for a half hour or so, she stood and brushed the straw from her fanny.

"I'm cold. I'm going to find something hot to warm up with."

"Use me," he said before his brain got control of his mouth.

Her cheeks pinked-up some, but her eyes said she was interested.

"Help me up," he said, reaching for her before she changed her mind. When she grabbed his hand, pulling him to his feet, he explained, "Among other things, my knee's stiff."

Their vehicles mirrored their physical differences. She drove a little compact car and he drove a big Ford pickup. She had to scramble onto the truck's running boards just to get into the cab.

He opened her door, refraining from giving her a boost although he wanted his hands on her heart-shaped ass more than he wanted air.

Chapter Two

EVIDENCED BY THE erection pressing against his zipper, Luke's little head was ready to fuck. But his big head, the one assigned to do his thinking, said no way was he taking her to his place for lots of reasons, the biggest being getting naked with her.

He'd had a few ventures in bed since he'd lost his leg, and none of the women had wanted seconds after they'd seen the mechanical extension and knee replacement.

Or maybe he hadn't tried hard enough. Hell, he didn't know anymore. It irritated him to think about women, ex-wives, failed relationships, and the difficulty of getting good sex—dammit—make that *any* sex.

The hope that something fine might happen disappeared and his mood soured. He prepared to swing through a fast food place and play dumb on the way back to her car—no harm done and have a good life, blue-haired girl.

But before he turned into McDonald's and began his retreat, Kiley took charge and Luke didn't have to do a damn thing the rest of the night but smile.

"I don't take men home with me and I don't go home with strangers. Are you interested in having sex?"

"Yep," he said gruffly. "Where to?"

She gave him directions to the local make-out site. "Got a condom?" she asked and not one to look a gift horse in the mouth, he pointed at his glove compartment.

"Some in there, I think." Then he wished he hadn't added the, "I think." She didn't need to know how long it had been since he'd needed one.

Condom in hand, she unzipped him and since he'd dressed commando, she had bare skin and aroused cock waiting for her. By the time they reached the edge of town she'd covered his dick with both the rubber and her mouth.

After two preliminary swipes with her tongue, she looked up at him and grimaced. "I hate the taste of these. Yuck."

He didn't know what the hell he should say to that. She didn't appear to need an answer but went back to work and he doubly appreciated her efforts knowing that the flavor didn't appeal to her. Covered or bare, his dick experienced heaven as she nuzzled and sucked. When she deep-throated him, lightning shocks hit his spine, radiating outward, and his chest ached at the effort it took to breathe, drive, focus on the road, and not come.

"How far?" he muttered desperately.

Her hair tumbled loose, brushing his stiff penis as she looked up and out the window.

"Half a mile and turn, follow the dirt road to the bluff."

As he followed her directions, she returned her attentions to his erection, sucking him, corkscrewing her hand around his shaft and pumping his dick.

"Ease back on the seat so I can reach you, sweetheart." When she lay next to him, he urged, "Let's get your pants off, underwear too."

Without losing her place in his lap or her grip on his cock, she lifted her hips to help him and he shoved her jeans down far enough for her to get one leg free.

She made a noise in her throat, tickling the head of his dick as he slid his free hand between her legs, fingering her cleft and stroking the shell of her sex, before plunging into her wet heat.

"Oh God," she moaned around his cock, her hips coming off the leather and her thighs parting, inviting him deeper. By the time they parked, she'd unbuckled his pants.

He looked around, scanning the area carefully, not interested in putting on a show or getting arrested. It already amazed him that he'd driven from Doug's place to the local kids' make-out site with her mouth plastered to his cock.

At thirty-four he was a little old for high school shenanigans. But he had tinted windows, they had the place to themselves, and his cock stood tall, begging for more.

Liquid heat coated his fingers as he played in her slick folds while her lips surrounded his shaft, giving him back molten, pulsing pleasure.

"I hope you can wait for just a minute," she said, coming up for air when he parked. "Bring your butt over here and lift up."

"Yes, ma'am," he agreed, scooting from under the steering wheel, thanking God and good sense for not buying the bucket seat model of pickup trucks.

As ordered, he raised his ass off the seat, admiring her no-nonsense approach when she grabbed his waistband and took his pants to his hips.

"I need this," she explained, pushing his shoulders against the back of the seat and straddling him.

Luke stared in awe at her, wondering if he'd just been kidnapped by a crazed nymphomaniac. Not that he was complaining.

Primed and fighting his climax, he felt sweat dot his brow and gritted his teeth to keep from coming while Kiley inched her pussy down his erection.

He hoped he didn't look as thunderstruck as she did when she'd totally sheathed him.

"You're a fucking miracle," he muttered as her mound brushed against his groin and her sex kissed him, sucking on his length as hard as her mouth had.

She'd had her eyes closed but they came open at his words. If he was any judge, she was someplace between ecstasy and pure bliss. He flipped on the interior light to better see her expression.

"Hey," she protested.

"Tinted glass, nobody here, I want to watch," he growled. He held her hips, thrusting upward.

"Oh my God." She dropped her complaint, grabbed his shoulders, holding on at the same time she splayed her thighs wider, asking for more cock.

Luke was pretty sure he'd never been so appreciated.

She inched upward, stroking and clenching around his dick before lowering herself in a hip-swiveling motion that made his balls tighten as she rotated her pelvis, dragging the lips of her sex against his groin.

He laid his hand on her stomach and gave her another jarring thrust. Swear to God he felt long enough to reach high inside her belly.

"I need these." *These* being her tits, he made fast work of pulling her shirt high and her bra down enough to free them. When he tongued the first nipple, she clasped his head, arching her back into his mouth.

Being a man who thoroughly enjoyed the feel of female taut flesh between his lips, he didn't hold back, sucking, biting, and thoroughly worshiping her breasts.

He took her nub between his teeth, scraping the stiff peak with a rough caress and drawing on it, extending its length until she whimpered.

He reached between them, rubbing her clit while Kiley arched her back, put her hands on his shoulders, and closed her eyes, her hips dancing an erotic rhythm, rocking his cock deeper with each movement.

"Oh God yes…" she whispered, begging him to continue, "please."

Luke leaned against the seat, gazing at her as she took all the pleasure he gave her and reached for more. He wanted to watch as she came apart for him.

He swirled his finger in her wet heat and she opened her eyes, holding his gaze. Her channel pulsed, stroking his cock as she rotated her hips and then lifted high. He bucked under her, thrusting through clenching pussy muscles as she began her slide down.

"Come for me." He pinched the sensitive bundle of nerves, urging her to fly apart.

"Oh, baby," she moaned. Goose bumps raced over her body and a surprised expression flitted across her face.

Luke watched her begin the wildest hip-swaying, pussy-clenching orgasm he'd ever experienced. The whole time, she stared at him from half-closed blue eyes, her lips parted, her breath huffing out in excitement as she took her pleasure on his cock.

"Sing it for me, sweetheart," he growled as she climaxed and made the prettiest keening sound he'd ever heard.

"Come on, baby, give me some more." He sucked her nipple, gripped her rump, and held on as she clenched her sex, milking his length for the ride home.

"I'm gettin' close," he warned her, abandoning her breast to pull her mouth down. He kissed her for the first time, liking the flavor of her lips and the way she opened for him, taking his tongue as deep as she took his cock.

Ahuh, ahuh, ahuh... Both of them panted, making a commingled noise of pleasure as he lost the last vestiges of control and rammed his tongue down her throat and his cock inside her.

He held her breasts in his hands, squeezing them as she pole danced, riding his hard length with the tightest clenching muscles he'd ever felt.

Sweet fucking fuck. Tighter, tighter, tighter... He couldn't tell where his body left off and hers began.

"You like that, soldier boy?" she gasped, pulling her mouth away from his, then dipping back in for another deep kiss as she swiveled her hips, grinding her pelvis against his.

Holy fuckin'... "I need you under me," he grunted.

She accommodated the hell out of him by wrapping her legs tight around his waist as he grabbed her ass and hauled her higher.

With his fake knee anchoring him to the floor, and the other riding the edge of the seat, he began plowing into her heat.

She clung to him like a limpet, arching into his thrusts and moaning her enjoyment. Moments, hours, he couldn't say later how long before his body uncoiled, sending him spiraling into pleasure. After his last spurt ended, he collapsed, gasping for breath, his body splayed over her, pinning her to the seat.

If he hadn't felt so damned good, he might have been embarrassed. His cock wilted, and she stirred, blinking unfocused eyes up at him. A moment later her gaze focused, and she pushed against his shoulder, urging him up and off her.

"Damn." The windows of his truck were steamed over. Luke helped her untangle their body parts, though he didn't want to let her go.

"I need to go home." She didn't waste any time cuddling with him after she got her senses back. Though he only had to dispose of the condom, pull up his pants, and buckle up, she scrambled to find her clothes and beat him dressed.

On the trip back to Doug's place, she sat on the seat, her hands folded primly in her lap. Even though he'd aired out the cab, he inhaled the erotic mix of sweat and sex.

Other than that, it was hard to believe that they'd both gorged on lust moments before. He couldn't tell if she was regretting what they'd done or was too sated to talk.

He didn't have a clue what to say, so he didn't say anything until they'd almost reached her car.

"I'd like to see you again." As soon as he said it, he wanted to retract the words. "But, I don't really have time for a relationship." The man who had nothing but time on his hands tried to make his life seem busy. "When I'm not working I'm thinking about working."

That sounded pompous as hell and he floundered, knowing he was blowing the moment and dammit, he didn't want to. He looked at her sideways before pulling her closer, sliding his arm around her shoulders so her body rested against his.

Risking a quick glance from the road to look at Kiley, he took in her swollen lips and flushed cheeks. She laid her hand on his thigh, and he liked the feel of her palm there.

"I'm busy, but that doesn't mean I'm a eunuch," he amended.

"Duly noted," she agreed, patting his leg as she gave him a speculative look. "I'd also like to do this again."

She squeezed his thigh and it didn't surprise him when his cock stirred, already half aroused and ready for more of her. "Maybe we can help each other."

He didn't know what she had in mind, but he'd listen to find out.

"I'm a single mom. I don't have a steady man because I don't want one hanging around my two kids who are right now with my mom. She doesn't babysit often and aside from Marcie, I don't leave them with anyone else. I have a full-time life that includes a job and no time for a relationship."

"And?" He squeezed her shoulders, urging her to make an offer he wasn't going to refuse regardless of what it was.

"And—I have certain biological needs I'd like to satisfy with something other than plastic." She closed her eyes, her blush denying the intimacies they'd just enjoyed at the same time her hand stroked his thigh, promising more.

"Well, as to those biological needs—seems like we can find a way to get them satisfied. When you've got the time, I'll find the place."

He pulled up next to her car and put the truck in park, idling in front of her sister's house, waiting for Kiley's answer. When she remained mute, he decided coaxing was in order.

"You do the calling," he said, switching on his truck's overhead light to meet her gaze.

"I'd just as soon the whole town not know we're carrying on," Kiley murmured, her blush turning her pink cheeks to ruby.

"Carrying on?" After the uninhibited fucking they'd just engaged in, her old-fashioned description made him smile.

"Phone," he said, palm up, waiting. When she handed it over, he inserted his number into her contacts. "If you change your mind and don't call, it's okay. I'll not bother you. If you do call, I've identified the number as TF."

"TF?"

"That's military speak for *taboo frequency*—a line always open for emergencies. You call when you're able to get free and I'll make sure we get together."

He let her get half out the door before he added his last addendum to their deal. "As to the plastic, you might want to bring it along for a ride or two. No sense in letting it feel neglected."

He liked a little variety in the sheets and he figured he'd let her know up front, he wasn't all vanilla. He had a feeling neither was she. It wasn't a deal breaker, but he used the thought of playing with her toys to get her past the *would* she call to what they would do *when* she called.

"Maybe," she murmured, her cheeks even redder as she climbed from his truck.

He set a record getting his door open and to her side. He made it in time to lift her from the running board to the ground. She gave him a noncommittal nod as she unlocked her car.

As he stood watching, she slid inside and fired up the engine. Before she drove away, Kiley rolled down her window and whispered for his ears and not the neighbor's.

"Maybe."

He might have made a big mistake, but he'd been leaning against his truck, and stood up straight at the half promise.

"Don't get in a twist, but I'm following you home."

"Absolutely not." She looked horrified.

He stepped closer and bent down to her window. "Your need for privacy, I get. I'm cool with it. But not with you jumping in your car to race home alone on a dark night. I have a rule. If I'm sleeping with a woman…"

He paused, "Make that, when I'm fucking a woman, at

least at night, I see her back to her place to make sure she's safe. If you can't live with that, forget about anything else."

"You're not coming in."

"Did I ask to come in?"

He'd definitely ruffled her feathers with his rule. Nevertheless, he followed her to the end of her drive and waited for her to go inside.

Luke felt damned good on his ride home—better than he had in a long time, in fact.

Christmas tree farmer. He snorted at the idea, but still, it had him thinking about the stand of blue spruce on his property. It had been featured in the realtor's listing and when he'd taken possession, it had been one of the first places he'd visited when he'd walked the property.

I'll buy a 4-wheeler someday, but until then my feet will have to do. Make that one foot and a metal replacement…

Every damn thought ended up chasing back to the same place. He'd gotten his fucking leg half-blown off in the war and…

And that thought made him want a drink. Instead, he sucked in his gut and concentrated on the stand of blue spruce.

I don't know a damned thing about growing trees. But then again, apparently the ones on his property had grown themselves. He mulled over thoughts of trees and commerce during his trip home.

Somehow the sex had cleared his head, helping him think things through like nothing else.

He could see now that he hadn't been doing anything

other than coasting along, too apathetic to think even about selling.

He'd wanted land and liked the privacy of the place. Even the mail delivery stopped at end of the lane by the main road. But during his time here, he'd been drifting, as if waiting for someone to tell him what to do next.

"Sonofabitch." As he drove up the lane leading to his property, his headlights spotlighted the raccoon trying to pull the lid off his trash can. Caught in the act, the animal sat on his haunches, staring balefully through the dark at him.

Ready to do battle, Luke parked, left the lights on and engine idling as he opened the door, swinging down fast from the truck. The raccoon fled. It wasn't the first time Luke had chased off the varmint but although he could scare him some, nothing kept the pest away for long.

I swear if I have to sit out here and bang on a pan, that damned bandit will go hungry tonight. Baring his teeth in victory, Luke paused by the trash can, making certain the lid was strapped on.

He'd fought with the raccoon through the end of winter and into the spring. This round belonged to him.

Cheered by his immediate victory, Luke went back to the truck, reached into the cab, and shut off the motor. By positioning the trashcan by the drive, he'd fixed it so he could keep score in his battle with the ring-eyed nuisance.

He could easily check the status of the container from the porch. And when driving up his lane coming home, Luke sighted the can before all else, inspecting it for damage and plotting retribution if such occurred.

"Have fun, buddy. Tomorrow I'll move the can again." As quick as Luke issued his challenge, damned if the animal didn't chitter his answer, apparently readying for his next shot at the can.

"I need to take this place in hand." Luke tidied the yard, determined to at least make the pest wait. The animal paced at the edge of the woods, clearly impatient for the moment he could get back to attacking the trash can.

At the VA hospital, the shrink had explained soldiers were trained to take orders and had to relearn individual thinking. Luke admitted that until recently, his thinking had pretty much been confined to strategies for discouraging a raccoon.

"I'm overdue to quit farting around and deprogram myself." That settled in his mind, he finished repositioning his two Adirondack chairs and went inside.

"I need a life," he grumbled, but the image of Kiley popped into his mind. "No, you need to get laid more often," he answered himself, captured by an unfamiliar playful mood.

From his doorway, Luke scanned the area and mentally marked where he'd drag the trash can the next day. His less than profound mutterings accompanied him through the house.

He wrapped his lower leg in the waterproof cap and showered quickly, standing in front of the mirror afterward, studying his face and wishing again he'd trimmed his beard closer before he'd gone to Doug's. Without analyzing his why, he watched his lips curve into a satisfied smile—a smile he actually felt.

"I hope to hell she doesn't erase my number from her cell or have second thoughts about what happened tonight," he muttered, toweling his hair dry before throwing the cloth aside and climbing into bed, where he stroked himself absently as his thoughts played over the evening.

Shit. She came so many times I lost count. He groaned and licked his lips, remembering the flavor of her sweat.

I want a taste of her honey next time before I ride her pussy and suck her tits. The fact that another meeting had been left up to her didn't lower his anticipation.

He brushed his tongue against his teeth, trying to recall the exact feel of her taut nipple in his mouth. He'd bitten it lightly, scraping his teeth over the tip before sucking with hard pulls on her stiff peaks.

The memory made him hard all over again and he palmed his shaft, squeezing as he remembered the feel of her lips on his cock.

"Holy shit," he groaned, his hips coming off the bed as he grabbed the discarded towel in time to catch his release.

"Hell yeah, she'll call. It was her idea." Having a fuck-only relationship worked fine for him. He fell into a deep dreamless sleep that lasted until morning; birds and the sound of the trashcan tipping over woke him.

His first thought wasn't about raccoons or reconnaissance, though. *I need to get some better-flavored condoms.*

It didn't take him long to be up and out of the house, heading toward the spruce woods, navigating across the rough ground, matching the stride of his healthy leg to that of the titanium tube attached to the microprocessor knee.

Luke assured himself that wearing long pants and walking on flat ground, nobody would ever guess. His custom boot disguised the absence of a flesh and blood foot.

He cut through the overgrown field thinking about the night before and planning more occasions of Kiley fucking. Picturing her on a mattress—naked in a real bed, he stumbled, his smile changing to a frown. He would also be expected to shed his clothes.

Chapter Three

W*HAT DID I do?* Kiley woke up in her bed and lay staring at the ceiling, feeling one part satisfied and two parts appalled as memory washed over her.

Then she snickered, her giggle resounding in the bedroom. *Well, no, make that two parts satisfied and...*

The kids were at her mother's, which meant she had the house to herself and could lounge for a while.

The night before had been incredible. Moments of complete freedom didn't happen often. When she'd made it home, she'd planned on pampering herself. Bath, bubbles, candles, book, glass of wine and...

Kiley brushed a stray strand of hair from her cheek and exhaled, remembering. Tired and relaxed, she'd skipped the bubble bath, opting to stand under the shower and scrub her skin, inspect the red passion marks on her breasts and soap away the smell of him still clinging to her body.

The latter task she'd performed almost reluctantly, holding thoughts of him and their truck tryst at bay.

Clean and content, she'd slipped beneath the blankets, curling on her side in a fetal position, sliding her hands between her thighs for comfort. She'd closed her eyes and slept a deep, dreamless sleep like she hadn't experienced since before Evan died.

Remembering everything, her thigh muscles tightened, and her womb clenched. She hadn't needed wine to help her sleep. She'd just needed a bed.

She closed her eyes, trying to replay the ending of the evening. She hadn't needed to glance at her rearview mirror to know he was behind her.

She'd *felt* his presence in a weird kind of way. Her attempt to keep him from following her home hadn't worked.

"It's a stupid waste of your time." She'd tried one last volley, but he'd shrugged, climbed in his truck, and leaned out his window this time.

"It's late. Let's get this show on the road. You're going to an empty house. I'll tag along."

She'd felt a mix of exasperation and relief when, behind her, she'd seen his lights turn onto the unpaved gravel and his truck wait by her mailbox, engine idling while she parked her car, and unlocked and entered the house. She'd watched from her kitchen window like a schoolgirl as his taillights had disappeared. But she'd felt safe.

Of course, I always feel pretty safe here, escort or not, so I guess it was nice but not necessary. I'll tell him so. She grimaced at her assumption there might be a future conversation with him on the subject.

Before she could question her motives, she retrieved her cell phone from the bedside table and checked to make sure the entire evening hadn't been a dream. Just as he'd said, she found a new entry marked *TF* in her list of contacts.

Taboo Frequency… It didn't sound like a military term.

It sounded like kinky sex and made her lips curve in a satisfied smile.

Awake and hungry, her stomach growled, reminding her to get up. She swung her legs from the bed, pulled on a robe, and padded barefoot to the kitchen.

"Good God, I feel sexy." She rubbed her stomach and then pressed her palm against her lower belly at the same time her womb clenched.

"Who knew thorough familiarity with a male body could make such a difference."

Kiley made cocoa, filled her mug, and rinsed the pot before carrying her drink into the living room and setting it on the side table. Staring out the window at the mailbox at the end of the lane, she frowned, remembering how he'd waited there, watching her safely inside.

"But I told him not to follow me home." It smudged the fantastic evening and made her frown. She didn't want him dropping by.

"I'd like to just be able to fuck, dammit," she muttered, then realized how childish she sounded. Still, she'd had too many of her mother's boyfriends coming and going in her life as she'd grown up. She'd not repeat that mistake with her own kids.

Evan and Emmy weren't going through the same thing. No *good-time lovers* here today/gone tomorrow. Examining the twinges and aches in her body, she linked each one back to the cause: Luke.

She hadn't offered him her number, but it would be easy enough for him to get it from Doug. If he blew up the phone calling her or showed up on her doorstep pestering her, she'd stop him cold. But if he didn't, if he kept his part of the bargain and made time for sex with her when she called him, well…

"*Yummm.* I'll take him for breakfast every morning." She groaned, leaning back against the couch pillows, reliving the exquisite feel of his cock inside her, his teeth on her nipples, his lips and tongue invading her mouth.

"All that in a frigging pickup truck parked at Bindle's Bluff." Finishing her chocolate, she licked her lips, remembering Luke's salty essence instead of the rich cocoa taste.

Then she made a moue of disgust, comparing his spicy musk to the noxious taste of the condom material. "I'll buy different flavors."

Little by little, she mentally shifted to accommodate the possibility of a future for the bargain she'd made.

✧ ✧ ✧

HER LUSCIOUS MOMENT of solitude ended when Marcie, accompanied by her two kids, brought Kiley's twins home.

Thankfully, it was a nice day. As soon as they all climbed out of the car, the four cousins headed for the swing set in the side yard. Unfortunately, Marcie made a beeline to the house.

"What do you want?" Kiley stopped her sister at the door, not letting her in from the porch.

After Marcie held her finger on the doorbell, making it chime continuously, Kiley relented.

"Grow up," she snarled as she unblocked the entrance

and Marcie surged into the living room.

"Well, how was it?" Subtle, her sister wasn't.

"We went for a drive in his truck." Avoiding her twin's gaze didn't stop the blush creeping up Kiley's neck and heating her cheeks.

"It was a long ride. He didn't bring you back until two o'clock."

"Tell me you weren't standing by the window, your nosey nose pressed to the glass waiting for me to get back." Kiley glared at her sister.

"Doug's nosey nose, this time. I think he was worried about Luke."

"What? He thought I would attack his friend? You can tell him that Luke was just fine when he left."

"How fine?" Marcie circled back to her original question like a terrier after a rat.

"Would you stop?" Kiley snarled, willing her twin to leave her alone. "We are not in high school anymore and it's not show and share time. Drop it."

"He was that good, huh?"

"We drove around, we talked. No big deal."

"Better cover the hickey on your neck if you don't want Mom's third degree. I didn't squeal on you but between the whisker burn on your jaw, swollen lips, and strawberry mark I'm not sure how you'll convince her it was a platonic drive."

"I don't have to convince Mom of anything. I knew it was a mistake to leave the kids with her last night."

"Damn, Kiley. You'd think Mom was the enemy or something. Would you quit with the drama? She loves the twins just like she loves me and you."

Marcie slung her arm around Kiley's shoulders and gave her a squeeze. "I'll hush. I just want something good to happen for you."

"I think I'm getting a raise at the factory, the kids are doing well, both made the B Honor Roll at school, my bills are paid, and there's food in the cupboard. I'm doing fine."

"Kiley, quit dodging the issue. Did he kiss good?" Marcie beamed at her, grinning like a loon.

"Yes," she caved and answered. "He kisses like a pro— like a man who's spent time perfecting his talent." She let her analysis dangle in the air, tempting Marcie to spill her guts about anything she might know.

"Luke keeps to himself. I was surprised to see him last night. I don't think he's a player. Not since he left a leg in Afghanistan, anyway."

"What?" Kiley thought she must have misheard.

"I guess you really didn't do more than a little kissy face if you don't know that Luke's left leg is fake from the knee down."

Kiley stifled her urge to ask questions, hiding any reaction but irritation from her twin. "Marcie, you act sixteen, not twenty-six. He seemed like a nice guy. As for anything else, I'm not interested in a relationship and neither is he."

"Just saying," Marcie muttered, holding up both hands as if surrendering. "If you ever get naked with him, I don't want you to freak out."

"Duly noted. If we ever get down and dirty, I promise to not scream like a little frigging girl."

"You *are* a little frigging girl." Marcie grinned, bumping her shoulder against Kiley and pointing out the obvious difference in their height. Marcie stood five foot nine in her socks and Kiley barely measured five foot two. They were twins, but they really didn't look alike.

Except Luke recognized our similarities immediately and that means he had to be studying me. The thought brought a warm flush to her cheeks.

"No coffee this morning?"

"Hot chocolate." As soon as Kiley said the words, Marcie grinned.

"Pampering yourself today, huh?"

"Marcie, what do you want? I've got things to do that don't include your idiocy."

"Mom wanted me to check up on you is all. She saw your car coming home late and she wanted me to make sure her little girl is safe." Marcie cast a sly look at Kiley. "She said she saw a dark vehicle following you when you drove past."

"I knew better than to rent this place when I moved home."

"It was this or move in with Mom." Marcie flashed her usual smile and laughed. "Country living comes with tender, loving care. Did you forget?"

"Tried," Kiley admitted. She'd fled the place with Evan as soon as they'd graduated, intending to return only for holidays and short visits. But, eight years later, here she was again under the eagle-eye scrutiny of family.

"Thanks for bringing home the twins and giving me a heads-up." She switched to a safer topic. "I planned to stop by her house today, but I don't think I can face one of Mom's inquisitions right now."

She paused long enough to wipe off the table and look out the window where Marcie's two boys, Keith and Little D, played beside Evan and Emmy. "I had sex with him."

"Figured you did. You're smiling." Marcie leaned next to her, looking out the window too. "What's his place like?"

"I don't know."

"You brought him here?" Marcie's voice held shocked surprise as she turned from the window to look at the hallway leading to the bedrooms.

"No." Kiley grinned, still looking out the window. "The Bluff. We did it in the truck." Feeling sixteen again, she started giggling.

"No way." Marcie stared at her. "So, are you going out with him again?"

"He said to call him if I wanted to get together."

Marcie frowned at her in outrage. "You boinked and that was the best he could do? You didn't even get a meal out of it?"

"Oh hush. It's exactly what I want. No-strings sex with a man who doesn't want a relationship any more than I do."

Marcie put on a pot of coffee and sat down at the table waiting for it to perk. "So are you going to call him?"

Kiley rolled her eyes. "We'll see. I don't know. But I do know you need to keep your lip buttoned and not go telling Doug, Mom, or anyone else about it."

"Can't keep Doug out of the loop. We've got a bet going."

"What?" Kiley gasped.

"Doug bet you'd go for a drive and mess around some. I bet you'd go for gold. I'm collecting." Marcie's smug grin reminded Kiley why she should have kept her mouth shut.

"Do you two have nothing better to do than speculate about my life?"

"Nope." Unrepentant, Marcie poured the coffee and pelted her with orders. "Go see Mom. She's worried about you."

"You saw me. Tell her I'm fine."

"She babysat for you. Call her and say thank you. Tell her you'll stop by sometime next week."

"Marcie, you manipulated the whole thing. I didn't want Mom to babysit. I didn't want to go to your freaking Friday night firepit party. You made me do it."

"And you should thank me for Luke and a night of great sex, too." Before Marcie finally rounded up her kids and took them home, she teased Kiley with raunchy humor.

"Me, I like to roll over at night and sprawl on Doug. But you don't mind sleeping alone." She shrugged as if that was a sign of crazy in Kiley before continuing her instructions.

"Be up front with him about what you want. Most men can't find their way to a girl's clit unless she draws them a map."

"You are so crude." Kiley couldn't keep from smirking. Luke had that covered just fine.

"Someone already drew him a map, didn't they?" Marcie stared at her.

"Out, out, out. I'll call Mom. Promise." Kiley schooled her expression to indifference, waving her twin on her way.

Chapter Four

KILEY'S FIRST OPPORTUNITY to check out her sex-on-demand arrangement occurred on Sunday, when Marcie and Doug took all the kids to the movies.

She could have accompanied them. Instead, she'd no sooner dropped off the kids at her sister's than she called Luke's number.

"Luke here," he answered.

"I'm free for the afternoon." She felt a flush of embarrassment creep up her neck, waiting for his response, which didn't come immediately. But he must have been figuring out logistics.

"My place all right?" His gruff voice made her insides clench and she stifled the impulse to tell him the bed of his pickup would be fine. She should have been sated from Friday night's extravaganza but just the idea of seconds had her squirming.

"You'll have to give me directions."

"Do I get to continue that after you arrive?"

"Get me there first," she laughed. "Then we'll see if I can take orders." Fifteen minutes later, she pulled into the long lane leading to his house, wondering if she had lost her mind.

Instead of slowing her down, the question had her pushing the pedal to the floor, racing up the drive to experience the next dose of insanity.

She pulled in and parked in front of the house. No one stirred inside, so she looked toward the barn.

He walked out, bare-chested and gorgeous in nothing but sweatpants and tennis shoes. Lust thickened her tongue and made it hard to answer when he called to her.

"You ready to have some fun?"

"Oh, yeah," she murmured, climbing from the car. She expected him to walk toward the house. Instead, he motioned her to come to the barn with him.

We're moving from the pickup to the outbuildings? But she didn't protest when he led her into the darkened interior.

A mat covered half the area of the floor and iron rings dangled from the ceiling, clanging together as if he'd just released them.

Her gaze swept the big space, seeing a weight bench, exercise mat, rowing machine, suspension rack, and handgrips embedded on the climbing wall at the end of the room. He'd created his own personal gym.

"Nice," she muttered, walking to the edge of the exercise pad. Behind her the door shut, leaving only dim light filtering through high, dusty windows.

"Nicer," he murmured in her ear, placing one hand flat on her belly, the other cupping her breast. Even through the thickness of his sweats, the prodding of his erection against her butt left no doubt of his readiness.

She had no time to do more than draw breath. Sliding

his lower hand under her tee, he pulled it up and over her head, unfastening her bra at the same time with his other hand.

Chills of anticipation and bits of fear turned her nipples to hard nubs standing at rigid attention.

He dropped her shirt, brushed her bra straps down her arms, and pulled her bare back against his naked chest, cupping and caressing her breasts as he nuzzled a spot behind her ear.

Kiley couldn't hold back her moan. Her womb clenched so tight she felt the constriction in her belly, and the temperature in her core rose from simmer to burn.

"Want it?" he growled, pushing his hand under her waistband inside her panties, parting the lips of her sex, and stroking his fingers through her already drenched outer shell. He didn't need a map.

Kiley widened her stance and he found her hot button, rotating it with his finger. She ground against his calloused touch, at the same time feeling the press of his cock against her rump.

He slipped two fingers inside her, finger-fucking her with one hand while using his other to pull and tease her nipples, finishing her off when he bit her earlobe and pinched her engorged clit at the same time.

She shrieked. It felt so good, her body unwinding and her mind just letting go. Loose and recovering from her first orgasm of the day, Kiley stood docile and pliant as Luke stripped her shorts, panties, and shoes.

He didn't wait for her to revive, taking her to the mat

and positioning her head on her arms, her ass in the air. She heard him opening the condom package and smiled.

"My turn," he growled, swirling his readied cock in her wet heat, fitting it against her entrance, and sinking deep.

"Oh. My. God." Kiley spread her legs, taking all of him, feeling his jackhammer thrusts that scooted her across the mat.

"Gotcha," he laughed, putting a hand on each shoulder, keeping her from skidding away as he powered into her from behind.

"Spread wider," he ordered, and she did. He laughed and spanked one of her ass cheeks, making a loud slapping sound in the silent barn. Her channel walls wrapped around his cock, squeezing him lustily.

"Thought you'd like that," he grunted, slapping her other ass cheek a stinging blow.

She'd never considered a spanking erotic, but as he worked his cock in and out, teasing her clit, smacking her rear, and riding her pussy without stop, Kiley lost any inhibitions she'd ever entertained.

It felt wonderful cutting loose, grunting, moaning, and screaming her bliss each time another orgasm blasted through her.

He didn't pause, flipping her on her back and straddling her hips, facing her as he pumped her sex.

Her legs fell wide, letting him do what he wanted. He laughed, picking her up and holding her by the rump, draped her legs over his arms as he thrust into her in hard fast jabs.

Yes. Yes. Yes. Another orgasm spiraled from her womb, curling her toes and hair at the same time. She squeezed her channel tight, milking his cock as she felt the pulse of his release even through the condom.

"Hell, yeah," he groaned and collapsed on top of her, his penis buried between her legs, his face between her breasts.

Kiley drifted mindlessly in the space where huge roaring climaxes carry one. When she came back, he'd rolled them so they lay side by side, her head next to his shoulder, their hands entwined. She turned her face to look where he sprawled next to her.

"Howdy," he drawled, stroking the hair at her temple.

"Good afternoon to you, too." She giggled. It had been years since she'd felt like laughter and now in a matter of days, sex had her laughing like a fool.

He stood, threw her a towel and retrieved her clothes, dropping them next to her. She toweled the sweat from her body, washed her face with the wet washcloth he offered, and dressed.

He walked her to her car, opened her door, turning her to face him. Before she climbed in, he kissed her, his mouth a gentle caress against her lips.

"Call me anytime," he said gruffly, leaning down to speak to her through her window after she'd climbed in and started the engine.

Sheesh, I feel like an overcooked noodle. Kiley couldn't do more than nod. She needed to get home fast, take a shower, fix dinner for the kids, plan the week…

Who am I kidding? All I want to do is sleep. It wasn't until she actually went to bed hours later that she realized her afternoon lover had never removed his sweats.

✧   ✧   ✧

LUKE DISCOVERED FLEXIBILITY was the key to providing on-the-go service.

The third time Kiley called, he was on his way into Pittsburgh to buy a new mattress. He'd figured eventually, maybe, if all went well with Kiley, and God willing it would, one day she'd make it into his house and into his bed.

All the lumps and bumps in the old mattress he currently used suddenly became too pronounced to overlook. So, mid-week, he decided to drive into Pittsburgh, buy a new mattress, and maybe have it delivered by the weekend.

Since it was during her normal work hours, he didn't expect to hear from her. But when her number lit up, he pulled to the side of the road and got ready to play.

"Luke's takeout," he answered, grinning like a fool.

"Why does it sound like I'm on speaker phone?" she asked suspiciously.

"Because you're on speaker phone, sweet cheeks. I'm driving."

"Oh."

"What's up?" *Besides me.* His cock was ready to play, and that made him grin even more.

"Company's closed today for inventory. The kids are in school," she said in a rush, then went silent. Luke knew disappointment when he heard it.

"I'm on my way to the big city. Want to go?"

He could feel her thinking hard on the other end of the line.

Finally, she asked, "Where are you right now?"

"Getting ready to pull onto I-79."

"Go to the first rest stop and wait for me there," she ordered him.

"Yes, ma'am," he agreed. He was beginning to like this whole "let her be in charge" kind of thing.

It turned into a funny day, as in, he laughed every time he remembered it later. First off, she was into the whole Mata Hari thing.

"Do I look like me?" she asked right off the bat. Huge sunglasses hid her eyes, brighter than usual lipstick outlined her mouth, and a sunhat covered most of her hair.

"Nope. Now if you'd dyed your hair blue…"

She stuck her tongue out him, clasped her hands in her lap all prim-like, and asked, "So where are we going?"

When he told her they were going mattress shopping, she decided they had to be *strangers* in the store.

"How's that going to work?" he asked.

"We'll pretend we don't know each other. I'll go one way, you go another. I'll test the mattresses on my side, you do the same."

"So if I don't know you, how am I going to ask which—"

"We'll just wing it," she announced.

"Want me to drop you off a block or so away so no one can suspect we might know each other?"

"Don't be an ass," she told him and grinned, fairly

bouncing on her seat at the idea of playacting in the mattress store.

It took a while to agree on the right firmness for their needs. Especially since he couldn't concentrate on what was under him, for watching her, and wanting *her* under him.

By the time she'd improvised her way into *getting his opinion because he was just about the same size as her boyfriend*, his erection was pushing against his fly. The little devil gave him a sly grin and invited him to test the mattress with her.

"I'll take that one." He slapped his credit card into the clerk's hand, scribbled his signature without reading the bill, and leaned on the counter to hide his hard-on while he filled out his delivery papers. She went to the truck.

"Do you think he realized we're together?" Kiley asked as soon as Luke joined her. She'd renewed the color on her mouth, emphasizing his need to plant a kiss there.

"You're kidding, right?" As a matter of fact, the clerk had congratulated him on having such a hot girlfriend.

After she capped the lipstick, she dropped it in her purse and laid her hand on his thigh, patting him like he'd been a good boy. His cock jumped, trying to reach her.

"Want to get something to eat before we go home?" he asked, trying to be polite.

"Oh yeah," she answered, palming the bulge in his pants. "I'm feeling very, very, hungry right now." She ran her tongue over her plump red lips and Luke had to fight to control his release.

"You're going to pay for that," he growled. Shit, he had a wet spot on his denims where pre-cum had leaked through.

"So you say," she answered breezily, reaching for his zipper.

He didn't wreck the truck, they didn't get arrested. But... By the time he pulled into the rest stop where her car waited, he had a filled condom covered in lipstick stains to throw away.

She went to the ladies' room to tidy herself and Luke visited the men's. Then he visited the ladies' too.

"Always wanted to see the inside of a women's bathroom. Fancier," he told her, enjoying her flustered stare.

"You can't be in here," she said, ruining her scold by giggling.

"Best be quick. I propped a mop outside the door and put the 'Out of Order' sign up."

He turned her so her hands were on the sink and she faced the mirror; so did he. He pushed her britches down and told her, "Step out of one leg."

It was his turn to give her orders and she hurried to obey.

"Spread and bend," he told her. "I'm hard again just thinking about being inside you."

He sheathed himself and lined up behind her, but before he entered, he reached in front and pushed her shirt up. "I want to see your tits. Hold this."

Un-fucking-believable! He thrust through her wet, hot, folds and took her like there wasn't enough time in life to get enough. And maybe there wasn't.

"Squeeze your breasts, play with your nipples. Show me," he grunted. Thrust in so hard and deep, he lifted her from the floor.

"I can do better," he growled, taking a breast in each hand. "I wish I could suck on 'em right now," he whispered, humping up into her hard as he pinched her nipples. He settled for biting her earlobe and she went stiff in his arms, shivering all over as she came.

"Goddamn, baby," he told her, feeling her pulse and contract around him. He leaned over her, pumping his release into her and watching her face glaze with passion when they heard a clatter and a voice outside.

"Anyone in there?"

Luke handled things like a master. Finished, he stripped off the condom, threw it in the trash, zipped up, and exited the restroom while Kiley was still blinking at herself in front of the mirror.

"Best get dressed, sweet cheeks." He even took time to give her a pat of encouragement on her rump.

"Got a mess over in the men's," he said in explanation to the attendant who stood next to the "Out of Order" sign looking puzzled. "I dragged that out so I wouldn't have some woman walking in on me."

The attendant headed for the mess in the men's bathroom and Luke hotfooted it to his truck, not waiting to see if his story held. It wasn't a minute before Kiley followed him out and to her car.

As he watched, she tipped the car mirror, added more lipstick, and straightened her sunglasses. When she picked up her phone, he figured it meant, 'Over and out good buddy,' so he started the truck and got ready to leave.

"Forget something?" he asked when his phone pinged.

"You didn't say when *the package* will be delivered," she said, back in stealth mode.

"The eagle won't land until next week," Luke told her.

"Okay," she said and then added, "Thank you for the fabulous shopping excursion, Luke."

"You're welcome." And then he couldn't resist. "Over and out, sweet cheeks," he drawled.

She rewarded him with a huge smile, waved the phone at him, then answered breathily, "Over and out to you, too, secret agent man."

Chapter Five

KILEY'S LIFE TOOK a direct turn for the better. It was more than great sex, although sex with Luke Danvers made her see everything in a whole new way. She had Evan on the floor tickling him one night, when Emma jumped on too. They all rolled around on the carpet giggling.

"Why are you so happy right now, Mommy?" Emma's piping question made Kiley admit what had caused the change. All the fun she was having sneaking around with Luke Danvers. She hoped she made him happy because he made her want to sing.

"I guess Mom was chasing happy when we were growing up," she murmured to herself. "I'm not going to do that," she reminded herself firmly. "But, as long as it doesn't hurt the kids, it's all good."

After she'd rationalized her behavior into an acceptable form, she called in support.

"Mom," she said, ten minutes later after she'd rehearsed her conversation. "Can you pick up the twins and watch them after school tonight?"

"Of course. What's the occasion?"

"Overtime. Can't turn it down."

"Marcie mentioned you might be needing a sitter soon.

I'll start a project with the two of them in case you get the chance for more *overtime*, dear. Don't worry about a thing. I'll make certain they have fun."

Her mother's excitement at getting to babysit shamed Kiley for lying about why. Then she stopped feeling guilty when she recalled the gleeful tone in her mother's voice and her subtle emphasis of the word *overtime*. Marcie had shared.

Kiley made her next call to Luke. She knew he didn't trust her yet. He'd managed to keep his pants on the first three times they fucked. She figured he was never going to fess up to his war injury, and the longer he waited, the bigger deal it would seem, so...

⋄　⋄　⋄

LUKE DIDN'T TAKE Kiley on a tour of the house when she arrived. He ushered her straight into his bedroom, ready to show off the mattress they'd selected together.

She'd called him first thing in the morning to check on its arrival. Though he couldn't see her, he'd felt her bouncing with excitement. Which of course made parts of him bounce with excitement too.

"Can I come after work to see?" she'd asked.

"Hell, yeah!" he'd agreed, then started cleaning. He figured at some point she might look outside of the bedroom.

Halfway through the morning he got to thinking about his leg, or the leg he didn't have and almost called her back.

But since calls to her were taboo, not wanting to lose a minute with her, he devised a strategy that would keep him mostly dressed—again.

Sweats were easy to maneuver, so he showered and pulled on a clean set before she arrived.

Once she entered the house, he bear-hugged her, letting her feel how much he wanted her.

Without underwear to confine it, his loaded cock stood at full stance, nothing separating it from her but thin material.

"Good," he growled. "You wore a skirt." And what a skirt. Pencil thin, tucked-in blouse, prim and proper to the nth degree but sexy as hell with the three-inch heels she had on.

He walked her backward to the bedroom and then the bed. When her knees hit the edge, he hiked her skirt.

"Well, I'll be," he drawled, staring at her nether regions. A garter belt outlined her bare, shaved mound. "Sit."

Instead of dropping to his knees and risking a screw-up with his fake one, he tilted her backward, spread and lifted her legs over his shoulders, and parted the lips of her sex.

"Oh yeah, baby. Daddy's been craving this." Pearly cream lined her inner walls and he started his feast there. He licked up her honey, swiping his tongue from hole to clit. Even with her thighs blocking most of the sound, he could hear her shriek.

As distractions go, it was a pretty good one. By the time he'd mouth-, finger-, and tongue-fucked her to three climaxes, he figured she'd be too tired to do more than receive without looking too close at the giver.

When Kiley finally lay slack before him, her legs dangling limply over the bed, he shoved his sweats down to his thighs. He'd already rolled on a grape-flavored condom, so his rampaging erection was ready.

"I want to suck your cock," she said. "Lie down."

It wasn't quite what he'd planned to do next, but who was he to question the sequence of events. He sprawled on his back on the new mattress, his purple-covered cock waving high.

"Have at it."

Without the slightest warning, Kiley sat back on her heels and pulled his sweats down and off him.

Inside the rubber, his hard-on shriveled to a limp dick.

She rolled her eyes at him, elbowed her way between his thighs, plucked the condom from his flaccid penis, and set to work, bringing his bare cock back to life with her mouth.

"Holy Mother of God," he moaned as she licked, sucked, and mouthed his balls, a place no woman had ever gone before.

When she foraged lower, deep-throating him until he thought he'd choke just watching her, all he could do was writhe under her attentions and hold onto the sheets.

He forgot all about his damned leg while trying to keep his skull from flying off. She was the screamer, the noisy one, but it was he who threw back his head and roared when he climaxed this time.

He came so hard his hips jerked uncontrollably and his cock pumped so much seed she couldn't swallow fast enough. He'd propped himself up on his elbows, watching her giving him head, and when the cream spilled from her mouth, he came even harder.

Her hair, swinging loose, tickled his groin, making the act even more erotic. His fingers hurt where they'd clenched the sheets. He loosened them, continuing to stare at her as the last spasm of release rippled through his cock.

She'd smiled lazily at him, licking the last drops away before tossing her hair aside and wiping her chin on her shoulder. Her head continued the full turn, carrying her gaze to his knee and then lower.

"Pretty gross, huh?" he'd murmured, too sated to be defensive.

She ignored his oblique reference to his leg, her tongue flicking over her lips as if searching for more of his cream.

"Tastes a lot better than those grape-flavored love gloves you've been serving up."

He'd been feeling naked and exposed but when she'd cracked the joke, he laughed out loud and fell in love with her.

Maybe it happened earlier, but he was pretty sure that was the moment he'd always remember. The moment he recognized she'd given him a piece of himself back and he never wanted to let her go.

One thing Luke found certain after they'd tested and retested the mattress that afternoon. It was time to figure out a way to undo their agreement and redo it into a relationship.

Hell, she'd already taken ownership of his heart; he was ready to move her into his house.

✧   ✧   ✧

LUKE WAS OUTSIDE the next day when Doug made a trip to the farm, found him in the barn; and stayed to work out with him in his makeshift gym. The point of his visit soon became clear.

"Marcie says you're sleeping with my sister-in-law. That right?"

"I don't talk about women I might or might not be seeing," Luke warned him, one-part glad Doug had enough sense to be looking after Kiley, the other part wanting to snarl at his right to ask anything. "What's it to you, anyway?"

"Just making sure I won't be interfering with anything you've got going. Marcie wants me to fix Kiley up with a friend of mine who's coming to town. You know, do a double date. She's playing cupid."

Luke sucked wind, feeling as though he'd been punched in the gut. "Hell no, I don't want you introducing Kiley to one of your buddies."

"So you are seeing her," Doug growled.

"We've gotten together a couple of times," he admitted reluctantly, knowing full well that Kiley wanted her business kept private.

"Then why haven't we seen your truck at her house? You just using her?"

"Dammit, I'm not using her. Not at least any more than she's using me. We're fine. Leave it be." Luke felt frustrated enough to rip Doug's head off.

"Seems to me, if a man favors being with a woman, he isn't ashamed to be seen in public with her." Doug continued probing, ignoring Luke's attempts at discretion.

"Listen, dumbass. It's not me holding back," he finally admitted.

Doug pounced on his answer like a terrier after a rat. "Uh huh, that's just what I told Marcie. She owes me five big ones." He didn't bother to hide his smug satisfaction.

"Well, mind your own business. I like Kiley and she tolerates me. That's enough for now."

"Forget I asked. I'm just here to use your equipment."

Luke considered nosey a two-way street. Doug was a talker and by the time he'd worked his way through the equipment, Luke had learned a lot about Kiley and her family.

"She and her mom don't get along," Doug confided from the treadmill.

"Who? Marcie and her mom?" Luke concentrated on his arm curls, trying not to look at Doug's two legs.

"No, Kiley."

"Why's that?" Luke set aside the hand weight and gave Doug his full attention.

"Jeannie, Marcie and Kiley's mom, was widowed when the girls were eight, the age of Kiley's twins right now. Marcie says her mom had a lot of boyfriends when they were growing up."

"So? Did one of the sonofabitches abuse the girls?"

"I don't know. Marcie says not, but Marcie might've been lucky. Whatever happened, Kiley married early and fled the nest."

"I must have met her right after that." Luke grinned, remembering his first glimpse of Kiley. "She had blue hair, little silver balls in her right eyebrow, and a kid on each hip."

At Doug's questioning look, Luke laughed. "Endicott brought her to my marriage-break-up party."

"I remember that." Doug scratched his jaw and nodded. "Right after that, Endicott introduced me to his sister-in-law when she came to base for a visit. That's how I met Marcie."

"So you've known Kiley longer than you've known your wife?"

"Yes, but I didn't really know Kiley. She's not a talker like Marcie and her mama."

"Funny how they're so different." Red-haired and freckled, Marcie stood at least five-eight or -nine, with a rawboned, lanky frame. Kiley wasn't much above five two, with creamy skin, a sprinkle of freckles across her nose, lush curves, and a round ass that made Luke's cock swell whenever he thought about it.

"I've seen the family pictures," Doug said. "Marcie looks like her daddy. Kiley and her mama could be identical twins. Really odd when you see them together, which trust me, isn't often."

Luke grunted, showing interest without interrupting because he was a glutton for Kiley intel.

"Thank God, Marcie has her mama's personality."

Luke figured that meant Doug's mother-in law talked a mile a minute because Marcie chattered and teased nonstop. Kiley, on the other hand, was quiet—not counting bedroom moments when she came undone and screamed.

"You like your mother-in-law?" Luke asked.

"Yeah. Jeannie's a nice woman. When the shit hit the fan

and I ended up in a hospital room halfway around the world, Marcie dropped everything and flew there to be with me. Stayed with me until the first round of skin grafts were finished, and then traveled with me home to the VA hospital nearby. I don't know what I would've done without her family."

Doug frowned, rubbing the side of his jaw, where new skin grafts had left pink scars. "Our kids stayed with Jeannie and Kiley, so Marcie could be with me."

"Hell of a family." Luke cringed inside, recalling his own unheralded return.

The only thing he'd had pulling him forward and steadying him through pain had been a vague memory of owning a piece of mountain and some trees.

"Have you seen my stand of blue spruce?" Luke changed the subject, hoping Doug would have some marketing advice.

"Got something planned for the trees?" Doug set aside his weights, accepted the changed topic, and accompanied Luke to the copse of evergreens.

Once they arrived at the wooded area, Luke looked hopefully at the variety of different heights; some were too mature for an in-house tree, but others, ranging from three to seven feet, would be perfect by late fall for the holidays.

"Pretty," Doug acknowledged.

"Do you think there's any future in selling Christmas trees?" When Luke verbalized the idea nagging at him, he felt like a dumbass.

"Not really." Doug started shaking his head before Luke

finished his question. "People are going to the fake trees. It's easier."

He swept the area with his glance. "On the other hand, you could try letting them cut their own. Or assist in cutting their own."

Both men contemplated strangers using saws and Luke amended, "Maybe pick it out and help carry it back to the car after I cut it down."

"Or something like that," Doug agreed. "You'd need a website to advertise."

"Shit, I can't even get internet up here. How's that going to work?"

"I can't help you with the Christmas tree business, but I can get you hooked into cyber-world this weekend," Doug promised.

"I'm not sure what the hell I'm doing here," Luke admitted as they walked back to Doug's vehicle. Gloom settled back on his shoulders. He didn't owe on the place, but there would be taxes and upkeep, and he might need to add rooms… He needed an income.

"You'll think of something. Meanwhile, concentrate on Kiley. She's got two kids, a girl and a boy, both the spitting image of Endicott. They're a handful. She could use help raising them, even if she won't admit it."

"Kiley's in charge. If she wants things changed, she'll say so." But even as he assured Doug of that fact, he admitted to himself he already wanted a lot more than just sex with her.

Chapter Six

OUTSIDE THE OFFICE'S one window, November gloom darkened the skies. Inside, when the lights flickered on, then off again, Kiley sighed, pulling the flashlight from her desk. No surprise. The company had been having electrical problems recently.

"Maybe they'll let us leave," Kiley said louder than she intended. With the hum of computers and noisy machines silenced, her words carried to the other cubicles.

"Yeah, right. And I believe in Santa Claus." The disembodied answer floated in the air, dousing everyone's hopes with cynical reality.

Although there were intermittent suggestions that they all get up and walk out together, nobody risked it. Instead, they all sat in darkness waiting for permission to leave like school children.

Finally, Mark Harwell, the office manager, walked into the room carrying his own flashlight.

"Greeley says we're closing early," Mark informed them. "You'll all be paid full time for today. Have a good weekend."

Kiley scrambled just as fast as her coworkers, but most of them were already through the door by the time she grabbed her coat and personal items. Everyone hurried for fear the lights might come back on. If that happened, the decision to close might be reversed.

Kiley slid her purse over her shoulder and stood as Marcie peeked around the edge of the cubicle, pointing her own flashlight at the clock.

"Want me to pick up the twins when I get my kids from school? We're pulling taffy tonight and your two can help. It'll be fun. I'll bring them home after supper."

"Thanks." Kiley almost stuttered as she considered her unexpected windfall. *Two hours of my very own.*

She didn't waste time; sliding her cell phone out, she hit Speed Dial as she entered her car. *Please pick up, please pick up. Darn it. It's embarrassing how much I want him.*

She'd had sex with Luke on the brain all week and finally come awake in the middle of last night pulsing with the aftershocks of a dream-induced orgasm.

Their arrangement—sex with no strings other than she didn't sleep with anyone else and neither would he—had worked out fine.

They'd both gone to the doctor, been tested, and entered into an uncommitted commitment. She was on the pill, they used condoms, but once in a while they even went wild and fucked bareback, enjoying the amplified sensation and intimacy.

Gradually during the last six months, their stilted conversations that had been limited to, "I'm available," and, "I'll meet you," had morphed into real talk time when they lounged together in bed afterward.

When that happened, he'd keep his arm around her, rubbing her back while she told him twin stories. They'd made their arrangement in the spring and enjoyed it over the summer. It amazed her they'd been able to keep it going.

No doubt my overdeveloped sex drive has a lot to do with that. She still felt awkward when she let him know she was available. But, he'd said call him anytime, and for her, anytime was when she could steal a moment for herself, and that wasn't often.

Apparently, his trees weren't tied to a schedule because he always found the time to meet her. In all honesty, it wasn't nearly often enough to match her need, but it was the best she could do.

Anxious as a druggie looking for a fix, she counted the phone's rings, ready to hang up before it could go to voice mail.

She never texted him or left messages—both made their affair seem too intimate when in fact, it wasn't personal at all.

Early in the arrangement she'd trained herself to think about their encounters as therapy—with Luke the doctor on call delivering her meds. It was the clinical distance they'd agreed on—no emotional entanglements or expectations of anything more than what it was—sex.

He had his reasons and she didn't need to know what they were. She had her own issues. If she ever married again, the kids would have a father. If not—they'd have to make do with her.

She'd dated Evan all through high school. They'd been

sexually active after the third date. She'd gotten pregnant when they were both seniors. He'd given up college and gone into the military to get benefits for her. He'd hoped to go to college when he got out.

Regret gnawed at her sometimes. She figured subconsciously she'd willed getting knocked up because she'd wanted a family of her own so badly.

But had things been different, the twins wouldn't be here, and she couldn't regret them and neither had Evan. He'd been so proud of them. Remembering his words still brought a smile to her lips.

"Two babies," he'd bragged, thumping his chest dramatically. "I'm the man."

"You're still the man," Kiley muttered fiercely, reminding herself where her loyalties were committed. Although being a widow made her both father and mother to her kids, all that parenting didn't smother her desire for sex. Evan had teased her about it.

"You need it more than I do," he'd said, laughing at her when she'd pounced on him and dragged him to bed after one of his long absences.

He'd made it to private first class, gunnery specialist and he was proud of that too. Nobody had promised them forever, but... Evan had left her here in Waynesburg before he'd returned to Afghanistan the last time.

"You'll be among friends. It will make me a lot easier in my mind knowing that you and the kids'll be here until I get back." He'd settled her in a rented house close to Marcie and Doug's place and deployed with Doug the next month.

He'd come home twice during that deployment. The second time he'd been in a body bag. The twins had turned five that year. They knew him because she kept his memory alive. But, they hadn't really *known* him as a father.

She'd been alone except for his high school graduation picture since then. She kept it next to the nightstand and his dress uniform picture sat on the mantel in the television room.

She didn't need to look at either image these days to remember Evan. The twins looked more like their daddy every day.

She'd put the government death benefit in a trust for the kids' education. It was Evan's share of their future. She wanted them to grow up knowing that he'd provided for them even after he was gone.

Everything else was up to her. She supposed the trauma of Evan's death plus the necessity to find employment had quieted her normal sexual needs. Her desires had been manageable until her body had roared back to life after she and Luke had engaged in sex the first time.

The man filling her thoughts answered on the fifth ring. "Hey, what's up?"

"Uh, I have a spare hour. Maybe two." Her toes curled, responding to his rumbly tone.

"I'll meet you at my place," he answered immediately. "If you get there first, you know where the key is." She'd made it clear she wouldn't go in before him, but he always said the same thing, letting her know she was welcome in his world.

She dropped her phone in her pocket, her sex clenching

in anticipation. She liked his no-nonsense, straight for the action response. It suited her just fine. She needed hot, raw man-handling—right now.

His Ford F-150 already sat in front of his house when she parked her Escort. He opened the front door as if he knew she might lose her nerve and leave if he didn't show himself.

He always made her feel comfortable, like having sex with someone she barely knew was the most normal thing in the world.

She appreciated his attempt to make it seem less pragmatic. *The bottom line is, we have one mutual goal—physical satisfaction.*

"I was thinking about you when you called," he said gruffly.

She stepped through the doorway into the house, every nerve in her body tingling with awareness, wanting to be naked with him immediately.

"Likewise," she laughed ruefully, almost telling him about the hot dream she'd had the night before. She didn't have time, though; he leaned into her, his erection pressing against her belly.

He'd obviously been thinking of her as well. Any shy thoughts fled beneath the flood of lust pumping through her body.

"Oh God, yes," she moaned. Leaving reticence behind, she grappled with his zipper and freed his cock.

His already aroused length grew thicker and longer in her hand. Dropping to her knees, she closed her lips around his cockhead, needing the taste of him in their foreplay.

It was his turn to groan as she licked the drop of pre-cum from his slit and then sipped and suckled her way down his steel-hard length.

He stroked her neck, lifting her hair to the side so he could watch her take him this way. She hummed as she ran her tongue along the underside of his shaft, and he trembled as her throat vibrated around him.

"If you don't stop, we're going to fuck right here on the floor," he growled, pulling her to her feet. Maybe they would anyway, because he hiked her skirt to her waist and shoved her panties down.

Glad she'd worn her sexiest undies today—probably a result of her orgasmic dream—she stepped out of them and her shoes.

As he lifted her, she wrapped her legs around his hips, matching her pelvis to his groin so that he found her opening and slid home. She couldn't hold back her gasp as he tunneled through her tight folds, pushing his way to her core.

"Every time it's like the first time," he murmured gruffly, nuzzling behind her ear as he stroked in and out below. "You squeeze me like you've got a fist around me, sweetheart."

Her slickness eased his way, but he was so swollen with need, his cock tugged on the walls of her channel as he thrust into her.

She panted, accepting him, willing him to fill her, arching into him so that the head of his cock reached so high inside of her, it rubbed her sweet spot, making her mewl with pleasure.

Lifting her higher, he draped her knees over his forearms and spread her legs, pushing into her as he took her mouth in a deep kiss. When they came up for air, both gasping for breath, he cupped her face between his hands and stared into Kiley's eyes.

"Baby, you do things to me I didn't know could be done," he groaned.

"Come for me," he coaxed, brushing his thumb against her clit, the trigger that sent her into a cascading climax, spiraling them both toward nirvana. He watched as she closed her eyes and let herself fly, wrapping his cock in a stream of pulsing heat.

"Well, hello," she whispered softly, blinking back to awareness and meeting his heavy-lidded gaze.

He kissed her, slanting his lips over hers, his tongue penetrating her mouth as he began a slow, steady, pattern of thrust-withdraw both there and below.

She sucked on his tongue, tightening her feminine walls around his cock, signaling her readiness and need again.

Releasing her mouth to bury his face against her neck, he laughed. She pulled his shirttail from his pants, hastily claiming the bare flesh on his back. She wanted her hands on his skin when he came.

His lips found the spot where neck joined shoulder, sucking on her there as he began to deliver short, jarring thrusts. His back muscles grew taut under her fingers.

She gasped and clung to him, her second orgasm building into a crescendo release that joined his as he spilled inside her.

He kept her legs around his waist and moved with her to the bedroom. She couldn't remember later if they'd fucked again before they undressed or if their clothes had come off during the sex. They were both so desperate, it was a wonder the material remained intact afterward.

She would have loved to curl up and sleep when she lay sated in his arms, his hand stroking absently up and down her spine, but...

"Gotta go," she said, rolling free of his embrace. Belated modesty made Kiley pull the sheet around her as she sat on the side of the bed and dressed. Her lips felt pouty full, her thighs trembled with fatigue, but her feminine core purred with contentment.

Bet I sleep tonight. This was the part that she always found awkward. She could hear Luke buckling his belt and stomping his feet into boots.

"You don't have to follow me home," she said without looking at him.

"Just as far as the turnoff," he drawled.

They had the same conversation each time they parted after having sex.

✧   ✧   ✧

It HAD GOTTEN cooler outside during the afternoon. Luke started her vehicle, letting it get warm inside before she left for home. If it hadn't been for that, he knew she'd have run straight to the car and sped away.

He was trying to get a handle on expanding their relationship. Well, he called it a relationship. He knew for a fact that Kiley didn't see it that way. As far as she was concerned, she came to him when she needed sex—period.

Their arrangement had pleased him well enough when they'd met. Until he lucked into Kiley, he hadn't had the social skills or patience to find someone to fuck; nor was he inclined to tomcat around. But he liked sex often and figured a steady supply was better than hit or miss. Her offer had come at a perfect time and filled all his needs. Well, at first she'd fulfilled his needs.

In spite of the sexual satisfaction coating his bones, Luke acknowledged his growing tension as he followed her home in his truck. He waited by her mailbox, engine idling when she turned off the main road and drove down the lane leading to her house.

He didn't leave until she parked, and he saw her taillights flicker off. Then he drove back to his house which seemed even emptier now that her visit had ended.

He spent the rest of the day working in the barn, but her scent remained on his pillow when he returned to it at bedtime. Before he went to sleep, he curled around it, pondering the situation.

The truth was, he wanted more of her time, but she didn't have much to spare since she had kids. She told him wry stories about the trials and tribulations of raising twins, but her laughter didn't disguise her pride in them. He'd started thinking lately that he needed to get to know her children.

Had she tried to engineer a meeting between them, he'd

have taken the gesture as a breach of their agreement. Privacy had been a huge deal at the beginning. They'd both agreed to be nothing more than a steady source of pleasure for the other. Her personal life was off limits, as was his.

"I was a dumbass." Except for Kiley, he didn't have a personal life. He could see that now, but that didn't change the fact that she'd made the stipulation and he'd agreed. He'd changed his mind since. He wanted more than sex. But he wasn't sure how to proceed.

Chapter Seven

"SHIT, SHIT, SHIT…" Kiley stood in front of the sign, trying to keep from being jostled as others crowded around her. Evidently, the lights weren't the only thing going out last Friday. From either fear or the cool autumn air, she shivered.

It was Monday, and according to the posted notice hanging on the front door of the Bencher Footwear Factory, the business had closed and wasn't reopening.

"Damn," she muttered, holding her feelings of panic at bay.

It was ironic that it took this colossal piece of bad news to make her put things into perspective. She'd thought she couldn't feel worse; she should have known better.

Luke Danvers had dropped in at the house on Saturday and she'd been cold, ruthlessly sending him away. Well, okay, maybe not ruthless. She'd let him stay long enough to satisfy the kids' curiosity.

"Mom, there's a man at the door," Emma had yelled. Evan Jr. had slid across the wood floor in his sock feet, shoving Emma aside so he could do his eight-year-old version of manning up.

"Let me talk to him," he'd ordered his twin as Kiley

hurried to see who was at the door. She'd been stunned to see Luke standing there with his damn sexy grin plastered in place.

"Kiley," he'd said, crooking his eyebrow the way he did when he was being ornery. He hefted a pizza big enough to feed the Dallas Cowboys, and Cowgirls, too.

"What?" Duh, even remembering, she blushed at her blank astonishment. She'd just stood there staring at him until Evan had opened the door and ushered him in.

"You a friend of Mom's?"

The question had jarred Kiley into speech, and she'd taken charge. She'd been polite, introducing him to the kids as an acquaintance.

She'd always prided herself on her quick thinking. She'd said tartly, "I'm considering buying a Christmas tree from him."

That was a mistake. He'd opened the box of pizza and told the kids about the stand of blue spruce he was so proud of. He eyed her front room ceiling and then said to Evan, "I've got some real pretty seven footers to choose from."

They ate pizza and he told the kids about the buckskin mare ready to foal. After he tantalized them with thoughts of baby horses and mesmerized them with his gruff charm, he left. Emma immediately asked for a book on horses for Christmas. Evan was more to the point.

"Maybe we can visit. Will you ask?"

She'd wanted to punch Luke in the nose, right after she dragged him into her bedroom. Her reaction only proved she was a chip off the old block because that's exactly what her mother would have done.

"Pissed off, aren't you?" He'd called her later, breaking another rule.

"You're not supposed to call me. I'm supposed to call you."

"Well, as to that. Since you're mad anyway, what's one more black mark? I'm sorry for pissing you off." But he didn't sound sorry. "I've got to tell you, I figure it's time to take this thing we have a step forward, Kiley."

"Don't even go there. We have an agreement I'm happy with. You can't change it just because you say you can." It made her mad that he didn't even argue. Which she understood right off meant his apology had just been filler-in words without intent anyway.

His visit had been a wake-up call. She'd been fooling herself that it would work long-term. Before it became more tangled and her heart was involved, she'd decided to make the break permanent.

She'd slept little and had even been looking forward to the distraction of work to get her mind off her feelings of loss. So much for that.

Now she had a much greater problem to worry about and her emotions were an indulgence she could ill afford.

She had to work, if not at the factory, then at another job. Not wasting time ranting against the company management, she pushed through the employees still fighting to get close enough to read the sad news sign. Once she reached the back of the crowd, she didn't linger thinking about what had been.

I need to find another job fast. Fifty other unemployed shoe factory workers would now be vying for employment in town.

By the time she'd shouldered her way out the door, she felt decidedly sick.

"I'm going home and howl on Doug's shoulder," Marcie said, catching up with Kiley in the parking lot. "I've got the kids' toys on layaway and Greely better make good with the final paychecks."

That thought hadn't occurred to Kiley. Grimly, she contemplated the state of her bank account while Marcie's nervous chatter gave her more to worry about.

As she listened half-heartedly, Kiley's gaze skated over the parking lot, stalling on the Ford pickup. Luke lounged in his F-150 and saluted her with a cup of coffee. *What is he doing here?*

"We'll make do with Doug's check until I find something else. Not good, but we'll be okay. How about you?" Marcie's voice piddled to a stop as she followed Kiley's glance. She unexpectedly giggled.

"What?" Kiley asked self-consciously.

"Doug said Petey Nelson told him that he heard from someone that you and Luke were seeing each other." Marcie grinned at her without remorse. "Guess your secret's not so secret anymore."

Busted. Kiley looked at her and admitted weakly, "I should have seen it coming. You are such a gossip." Nobody with any sense told Marcie anything private because Marcie told Doug everything she knew ten seconds after she learned about it.

"How long you going to keep pretending you don't know each other?" But then her interrogation was cut short when Luke drove toward them.

"Never mind, catch me up later." Marcie hugged her, whispered, "Hot, hot, hot," and ducked into her Honda, leaving Kiley to face Luke alone.

"Picked up a spare coffee when I heard the news at the diner down the street." He dangled the cup between thumb and finger, teasing her with it.

"Well, now that you've got the whole town's attention, give it to me," she huffed, standing on her toes to reach through the window of the tall truck.

"Nope." He set the cup back in the holder. "You've gotta get inside with me if you want a taste, little girl."

"What are you, some kind of perv?"

"I could be." He wiggled his brows at her suggestively before he put the truck in park, opened the door, and stepped to the ground.

"I know for a fact you've got time to play this morning. How about you climb up in this big truck of mine and let me take you for a ride?"

"I'm out of a job, Christmas is around the corner, and I don't even have a frigging tree for the holidays, let alone presents to go under it—and you want me to play?"

As Kiley catalogued her reasons for despair, her heart lightened considerably. She stared at him, reluctantly entranced by the crooked grin accompanying his invitation.

"Yep," he growled, lifting her into the truck before she

agreed or disagreed. "Besides," he said slyly, "I've got a stand of Christmas trees, remember?"

"Don't you have work to do this morning?" she snarled, reminded of his idiotic behavior the Saturday night before. "I distinctly remember you telling the kids about all the work you do on your Christmas tree farm."

"You can help me with my chores," he answered glibly. "Buckle up, sweetheart."

✧   ✧   ✧

LUKE TRIED TO quiet the laughter rumbling in his chest. He was pretty sure if he let it escape, she'd club him upside the head.

Tension radiated from every line of Kiley's body.

"On second thought, we'll live dangerously this morning. Slide over here and let me rub the kinks from your shoulders." He reached across the seat and pulled her into the crook of his arm. She let out another huff that might have been a sob and scooted close, burying her face against his chest.

"Dammit, dammit, dammit," she cursed softly against his coat.

He dropped a kiss on the back of her head and cuddled her closer. "We'll be fine." He murmured the words against her hair, unequivocally counting himself in her life.

She was tough, his Kiley. He didn't know when he'd started thinking of her that way, but his heart had laid claim to her a while before his head had even realized it.

Now he guessed the cat was out of the bag, and she realized it too. But, she wasn't shoving him away, so that seemed promising.

She was quiet on the drive to his house. He didn't have much to say either, so he flipped on the radio and let Christmas songs play.

"That's my favorite carol," she announced as "The Twelve Days of Christmas" filled the silence.

She started singing along as Luke drove up the farm lane. He didn't switch off the radio until the final line played and Kiley sang, "And a partridge in a pear tree."

Truck shut down, he turned on the seat, getting both arms around her so he could hug Kiley tighter. "Come on, tough girl," he teased, rocking her in his arms. "Let's see if you can keep up. Lazing around that office every day probably made you soft."

He tried to keep his tone light and hide his lust, but he couldn't keep his hand from cupping her breast or hold back the groan that emerged from his throat. "Come to think of it, you are soft—in all the right places," he growled.

She was upset. He might want to knock off the jokes. He wanted her too much. It made him heady, almost drunk around her. Not just the sex—he craved her company. Hell, her opening volley had pinged with irony. There wasn't a time of day he didn't have her on his mind.

But then she reached under his shirt and pinched his nipple, making him jump.

"Yikes, your hands are cold as ice. Where's your gloves, honey?"

"In my desk, in the building that once housed my job,

the employment I no longer enjoy." She banged her head against his chest. "This is not good."

Luke captured her other hand and slid it under his shirt, shuddering when her fingers covered his lonesome nipple. "Feels real good to me, sweetheart."

They didn't make it to the house to fuck. She unzipped his jeans and peeled them down around his hips.

He scooted to the middle of the seat and reached under her skirt, tugging down her panties so he could get inside her when she straddled him.

"I'm going to need those pretty tits uncovered for me to suck." He choked out the words around a tongue that felt swollen with raw lust as she rubbed the seam of her sex over his cockhead, rocking a moment before sliding down on him, then clenching her inside muscles and squeezing.

He forgot about the seat being cold on his bare ass when she undulated her hips, rotating her tight heat around his erection.

He'd not been kidding her. He needed to suck her breasts, tongue her nipples, bite the turgid flesh, and lick her to climax.

He pulled up her sweater, pushed down her bra, and set his lips around the ruby tip pointing at him.

He'd been afraid he'd lost her with his impromptu visit on Saturday. She'd watched him with the kids like a wolverine with cubs. He'd been wrong in thinking she'd just let him waltz in and enjoy her family too.

He'd missed most of his sleep the night before, trying to think of a way to get back into her good graces. First thing this morning he'd decided to catch her before she went into her job. Maybe coffee and a talk would smooth things over.

He'd heard the news about the factory shutdown in the diner, like he'd told her. And it wasn't good news. And he was damn glad he'd been in the parking lot when she came out. She'd been a little shocky. He'd seen the look too many times to not recognize it.

She wasn't shocky now. She was molten heat in his hands. "I'm going to eat you up and make you scream when you come," he promised, rolling the end of her nipple in his mouth before covering more of her breast, taking the creamy flesh between his lips and pulling on it with strong suction.

The walls of her channel flexed, fisting around him tighter than a rubber glove and she moaned, the sound escaping her throat as Kiley tipped her head back, arching into his greedy caress.

She swayed over his groin, seating his cock ever higher as she pumped her hips up and down, pleasuring both of them. He let her control below as he feasted on her breasts, devouring first one nipple, then the other.

When she came, she grabbed his head and held on, pressing his mouth tight to her sensitive nub. He kept on sucking it, stretching the tip and tonguing it as the ripples of her release spread through her, acting on him as a siren's call, demanding that he follow.

He grunted, scraping the tip of her nipple with his teeth and sucking hard on it one last time.

She moaned, disagreeing with the move when he released her, pulling out of Kiley altogether.

He pushed the seat back before pressing Kiley to her knees on the floor. She rested her head and arms on the seat as he drew her rosy rump cock high.

Pushing his jeans down farther, he put more weight on his knee than he should have and winced in pain as he crouched behind her, afraid to touch his dick lest he lose control and shoot.

"I'm going to give you a good ride, now, sweetheart," he growled, surrounding her legs with his thighs. He played in her slickness, rubbing his cock up and down her slit until she begged him to quit teasing her.

He wanted to play longer. Knowing he'd last about two seconds once he put it inside, he sank two fingers into her, pumping his digits in and out, feeling her velvet sheath sucking on them.

"I need your cock," she moaned after he'd teased an orgasm from her.

He ran his fingers through her hair, tilting her head back so he could watch her break apart for him.

"Take all of me," he growled. "Milk it for me, Kiley."

She pulled his head close enough to bite his lower lip before licking it. He tangled tongues with her as her channel tightened around his fingers. He added a third as she squirmed and spread her thighs, inviting him to sink deeper into her tight, wet heat.

If he was hot, she was hotter. He finally lined up behind her and sank his cock, grunting with each thrust, and grinding his teeth to keep from coming.

"Do me," she ordered, and he dragged his thumb across

her clit, pressing on it as she writhed in response.

She went crazy, shuddering under him in an orgasm that made her pussy pulse and squeeze his cock. As he thrust one last time, prickles of ecstasy skittered up his spine as he spilled inside her.

Holding his weight on his arms, he stayed connected, his cock resting inside her sex. He knew the spot behind her ear was sensitive.

He nuzzled her there, breathing in their combined scent and liking the smell. "Ready for morning chores?" he murmured.

✧　✧　✧

KILEY'S PROBLEMS REMAINED on hold as Luke buttoned her coat and led her to the barn. Once there he instructed her on the way to pull a bale of hay apart. "One flake each." He pointed at the small section in her hand.

That job didn't take her long, since there were only two horses. One was dark brown, the other, lighter gold with dark mane and tail.

"What do you call that color?"

"Buckskin," he answered, scratching the horse's side under the mane.

"It's enormous." Kiley stared at the beast that seemed as wide as it was tall.

"Penny's not enormous; she's pregnant and ready to drop her foal any time now. Aren't you, girl?"

Affectionately he scratched the mare's muzzle, gave her a final pat, and left the stall. Picking up a pitchfork, he went to work lifting the dirty straw from the floor to the wheelbarrow he had waiting.

Kiley didn't have a clue what she should do, but she wasn't much for twiddling her thumbs and doing nothing either.

Luke must have noticed her unease because he pointed at the house. "Hot coffee and breakfast would taste mighty fine when I get done out here."

"Was that a hint for me to go cook?" she asked, feeling a grin curve her lips.

"I don't do subtle well, do I?" He winked at her as she left the barn. As she passed the truck, her face turned bright red and she thanked God there was no one around to see it. She deserved a red face—the way they'd gone at it in his pickup was scandalous.

She shrugged and admitted to herself she didn't care. Her day, week, and probably month were shot all to hell. Luke had given her a worry-free hour.

His easy manner and teasing remarks made her feel as if everything would work out. In fact, she remembered him holding her and telling her that.

She sighed, grimacing at her wrinkled skirt and blouse. She'd have to go home and change after Luke took her back to town.

The memory of her predicament returned. She needed to find a job and she might as well get started. She'd forgotten that fact this morning when Luke swept her along with him.

Chapter Eight

"PLEASE ASK DOUG to come over. I'll watch the kids for you and give you a night out." Kiley tried to think of more to offer as she groveled, begging to use her sister's husband.

"I'll ask and he'll come. I'll make him. But you need to bite the bullet and call a real plumber, schedule a lube job for your pipes and when he presents the bill, pay it. Doug says you've got bigger problems than a plunger will fix and that's where his expertise ends."

Kiley looked at the water dripping from the ceiling of her basement and shuddered. "I called the landlord."

"Probably couldn't get him. Mom says he's on a cruise."

"Reception was fine from ship deck," Kiley told her grimly. "He said get it fixed and he'd take it off my rent."

"And?"

"I did call a plumber and I did get an estimate. The guy stuck a camera down in the lines, waved it around, pulled it up and said the front pipe has tree roots growing in it and there's a broken section out toward the street. It'll cost me three months' rent to get it fixed. If I had that kind of money, I'd put a down payment on a house and buy my own set of troubles. As it is, I paid over a hundred dollars just to hear the bad news."

"Oh. Geez. I'll tell Doug, maybe he'll think of something."

Kiley hoped so. The first time her pipes had backed up, two weeks before, Doug had shown her the valve to shut off the water. He'd used the plunger and it had temporarily cleared the line.

The key word there is temporarily. Kiley stared at the mess that had once been ceiling tiles. Using the valve, she'd reduced the current flood to a drip, but she couldn't keep the water shut off forever. Right now, the kids couldn't even use the bathroom. Trying to keep from complete panic, she mopped the floor.

Her phone vibrated and recognizing Marcie's number, she answered, muttering hopefully, "Tell me Doug's on the way."

"Yes indeed, they're on the way," Marcie announced in a chipper voice. "Doug found a buddy who can handle minor plumbing issues. He's bringing him along." Her sister's words extended her a lifeline and Kiley clung to the phone. "Uh, Kiley, you might want to clean up. Doug's friend is hot."

"I'm interested in getting my pipes fixed, not romance," she muttered, shoving the phone in her pocket. Using the push broom to direct another pool of water toward the drain in the floor, Kiley looked down at her wrinkled shorts and shrugged. But she'd pulled on the shirt sans bra this morning and her nipples were showing through the cotton material. "I need to change."

Before her thought took action, the doorbell rang and she heard two sets of feet run across the upstairs floor.

"Tell Mom that Uncle Doug and the plumber are here," Evan yelled, relaying the information to his twin, standing at the top of the basement steps.

Kiley grabbed a towel from the laundry basket and draped it around her neck as she called to Emma. "Send them down."

Doug's feet appeared first, clomping down the stairs. Before she saw his plumber friend, she recognized the uneven tread of the man following behind.

"What are you doing here?" she gasped in horror, re-membering her face, naked of makeup, her baggy shorts, torn tee, and dirty towel around her neck.

"I know how to dig," Luke said, ducking to avoid thunking his head on the low ceiling.

✧   ✧   ✧

THOUGH DOUG HAD spent plenty of time in Luke's barn using his exercise equipment, he'd never visited the house, or knocked on the door—until today.

"I know a poor widow who needs her pipes cleaned. I thought of you immediately," he'd announced as soon as Luke opened the door.

"I'm not much of a plumber," Luke answered.

"You own a shovel?" It had been early morning and Doug's gruff tone had suggested if Luke didn't have equipment, he needed to go buy it.

Shovel in hand, Luke arrived at the needy widow's place

to find her in meltdown. He hid his grin, tickled to see Kiley's confusion. He had hang-ups, she had more. Doug's request today had been gold. Luke looked around at the sagging ceiling tile and wondered what it would take to get it fixed.

Miss Independent Woman needed some help even if she didn't like him coming to her place. She'd made it clear she wanted to maintain the distance between them.

But here he was and there she stood, squeegee push broom in hand, hair in a ponytail, and a perplexed frown vying with her deer-in-the headlight stare. Finally, she unfroze and pointed at the ceiling.

"I have a leak. You know how to do plumbing?"

"Some," he grunted. Luke didn't want to claim skills he didn't have but her desperate expression, linked to the water dripping from above, kept him silent on the subject of his limited knowledge.

While they'd been eyeing each other, Doug went back upstairs.

"I'm taking the kids home to Marcie," he called back down, interrupting the silence. "Emma's gotta use the bathroom."

"I told her to pee outside, Mom, like I did. But she wouldn't do it." Kiley's son added his information as he shouted at the top of his voice down the steps.

"Luke, I'll go pick up the pipe you'll need after I drop the kids off. It'll be an hour at least before I get back."

Luke grinned, watching Kiley's expression change from irritation, to relief, to consternation. Without waiting for comment, Doug herded the kids outside.

As Kiley and Luke listened, the footsteps crossed above, the outside door shut, and finally the sound of Doug starting his Jeep and leaving reached them.

"You have no bra on," Luke muttered as soon as the silence in the house above assured him everyone had gone. "How about panties? Let's see if you left those off this morning, too."

While he talked, he walked, backing her against the cement wall, capturing her hands when she pressed them against his chest and pinning her arms above her head with one hand.

"I love your belly," he murmured, using his other hand to explore. The cropped tee she wore stopped at her midriff.

Her baggy shorts hung off her hips, leaving an expanse of bare skin. His breath ruffled the fine hair on Kiley's neck as his finger traced a circle around her navel.

✦   ✦   ✦

"YOU'RE SUPPOSED TO be working on my pipes," she whispered, desperately reaching for outrage to replace the sexual thrall rapidly overtaking her good sense.

"Uh huh," he agreed, nuzzling along her jaw, inserting his foot between hers, nudging her legs apart. His hand drifted lower, toying for a moment with her waistband before ducking under to discover she wore panties.

"I think," he murmured, pulling his hand free. "I need a taste of this." He butted her loose shirt upward, latching onto one of her nipples with lips and teeth while his free hand invaded the baggy leg of her shorts, sliding his fingers under the band of her panties to touch inside her cleft.

All the time, his lips suckled her breast, drawing and licking and nibbling and biting until she hovered, gasping, on the edge of orgasm. He dropped her hands, pulled her shorts to her knees, and stepped back.

"Turn around and assume the position," he growled, and she felt the heat in her core turn liquid.

She didn't hesitate, kicking off her bottoms. He'd already unzipped his pants by the time she leaned forward, hands flat against the wall, legs spread shoulder-wide.

She stared straight ahead as he lined up behind her, giving her his luscious, thick cock, the force of his first thrust almost lifting her from the floor.

He put his hand on her belly, steadying her as he fucked, squeezing one of her breasts, pinching her nipple as he entered and withdrew, plunging in and drawing out slowly until she shook with need, every nerve in her body poised to uncoil.

His rhythm changed, and Kiley tensed. She could feel him gathering himself, his muscles growing taut, his breath louder as he fought for control. She didn't want to be left behind. "Not yet, not yet," she warned him.

"Now," he overrode her judgment, pinching her nipple and clit at the same time, his hips changing tempo and becoming short, fast thrusts.

She was in her basement, not his barn. Her orgasm swept over her and she turned her head, muffling her shriek against his arm.

He hadn't worn a condom since she'd started taking birth control pills and she shuddered, loving the feel of hot spurts of semen hitting her internal walls.

Her womb lapped it up, contracting and milking his cock until the last trickle of his release.

Kiley more or less collapsed, her arms shaking too much to continue bracing against the wall. Before she crumpled to the floor, he pulled out and turned her around.

They stood holding each other for a moment, then, he stepped back, tucking his spent cock back into his pants and laughing. "Pipes, right?"

"Right," she agreed, snagging her shorts with her foot, scooting them close enough to step into and pulling them up; and as it turned out, none too soon. The sound of the door opening above had her scrambling.

"Kiley, you down there?" Her mother's voice reached her from the top of the steps.

"I'll be right up, Mom. Don't come down. The stairs are steep."

"No, they're fine. Marcie said you lost part of your ceiling, I want to have a look."

There was no stopping her as she descended, talking the whole way down. By the time she reached the last step, Luke had taken up the squeegee broom and set to work, leaving Kiley, looking as if she'd just been fucked—which she had—to face her mother.

Never at a loss for words, Jeannie Ballard didn't wait to be introduced to Luke. She patted Kiley's arm, pointing at the ceiling and delivered more bad news. "You'll need to have your electric checked too. The wiring may have gotten wet."

Then she looked at Luke and said, "Can we hope you're also an electrician?"

"No, ma'am," he answered. "My skills limit me to clean-up and digging." He accompanied his answer with a sexy grin, making Kiley's heart beat harder at her mother's expression.

"You'll do fine, I'm sure, just fine." She beamed at him until Kiley nudged her back upstairs.

When they reached the top, her mother whispered, "Marcie's right. He's hot."

Chapter Nine

"MOM, MOM, MOM," Emily chanted, demanding Kiley's attention. "Come on. Mr. Danvers is here. He's ready to take us to find a tree."

Evan was already out the door by the time Kiley reluctantly pulled on her coat. "This is not a good idea," she muttered as her kids raced ahead of her to their ride.

Kiley wanted to "bah humbug" everything about Christmas this year. She knew it was a bad attitude for a mother with children, but between the higher cost of heating fuel and the dreary winter days, she'd have preferred skipping right over the whole season and moving on to spring.

The kids expected a tree and they were going to get one—a seven-foot evergreen from Danvers Tree Farm. She suspected that was why she was in a grumpy mood. She hated taking favors from Luke.

Before the shoe factory filed for bankruptcy, she'd already picked up temporary work as an office receptionist.

To supplement the microscopic paycheck, she thought about finding a second job, but the only thing she'd found was working the supper hour at the diner. Tips there barely justified leaving the kids with a sitter.

Doug had helped Luke build a website and advertise his

trees. It had shocked him as much as her when he started getting calls from people. He scheduled the time for customers to arrive, even jotted down what they thought they were looking for.

She'd helped him mark the tree heights one afternoon, so he could find the correct one without wandering through them all.

Recently, their clandestine meetings had been few and far between. Luke suddenly had a busy time of year. And she had no time at all. She missed the sex, his slow drawl, spicy scent, and sweet smile, but most of all she just plain missed spending time with him.

In moments of insanity, she yearned for impossible things—like his lopsided boots permanently under her bed and her head resting on his chest each night after they'd made hot, sweaty love.

Adding to her depression, she'd finally checked out the local tree farm, discovering that even the cheapest pine was seventy-five dollars this year. Luke had offered her one of his blue spruce, free.

She didn't want to exist on freebies or rely on him for help that could disappear. Plus, his trees weren't cheap; they were well-shaped beauties he could sell for a lot.

She felt guilty accepting the offer but buying a tree would mean eliminating even more presents from Santa's already short list. Kiley had stalled the kids as long as she could, but two weeks before Christmas without a tree, she was risking being labeled *Number One Worst Mom of the Year.*

"Kiley, I've got a couple nice trees left that need cutting this year." Luke had tendered his offer again when he'd visited the restaurant the night before.

"There's no sense in you wasting good money on buying a pine when there's a wood full of blue spruce at my place."

As soon as she'd served him his usual pie and coffee, she'd slipped into the kitchen, hastily grabbing her coat, determined to pick up the kids from Marcie's house, and avoid further temptation.

He'd caught up with her before she could escape.

She admitted to herself later that he'd smelled so good she'd wanted to pull him into the restaurant pantry and make up for lost time. Instead, she'd headed for the exit.

He'd cut off her retreat, walking her to her car as he outlined his plan. "We'll take the kids to my place tomorrow, let them run off their high spirits and throw a few snowballs and such. Then we'll cut down a spruce, load it in the truck, and bring home your Christmas tree."

In desperation and against her better judgment, she'd accepted his offer. Now it was tree cutting time and she reluctantly followed her ecstatic crew out the door, watching from the porch as Luke buckled each child into the backseat. Patiently, he held the passenger door open, waiting for her to join the expedition.

"Don't make them love you," she warned him gruffly before she slid into the front seat.

His left eyebrow went up and his eyes crinkled at the corners as he gave her a quizzical look. But he didn't comment during the drive.

The kids bounced with excitement and Kiley spent her time frowning at them in the backseat trying to quell their squirming anticipation.

Luke didn't say a thing, chauffeuring them silently through the winter day. When they arrived at his farm, he stopped in front of his house and said, "I'll be right back."

He went inside and returned quickly with a thermos and basket of food. "We might get hungry if the kids take a while finding the right tree."

"You've thought of everything, haven't you?" Kiley asked grimly.

"I sure hope so," he drawled.

She wanted to wring Luke's neck. He was giving the kids a perfect day they'd never forget. Her heart ached, knowing that it was a memory she'd always cherish, too. It was exactly the kind of thing she'd tried to avoid.

From the house, he drove them over a newly plowed path leading to a copse of trees. As soon as he stopped, Emily and Evan unfastened their seat belts, fumbled open the door, and ran through the snow.

Kiley followed Luke, listening to him as he crouched next to the twins explaining to them that trees looked smaller outside in nature than they did in a front room.

"You're about three and a half feet tall. I expect your mom won't want anything much over twice your height."

Demonstrating the size they needed, he held his hand high above Evan's head.

With his instructions in mind, Emily and Evan judiciously walked from one spruce to the next, studying their prospects. When they'd chosen, Luke brought out a chain saw, slapped on some goggles, and went to work.

Emily grew bored and drifted away, returning to pelt Evan with a snowball. He retaliated and soon they were playing in the snow, the adults forgotten.

When the tree came down, Kiley helped Luke drag it to the truck and load it. With that finished, he brushed the spruce needles from her hair and said, "It's hot chocolate time."

Looking at him with exasperation, Kiley sighed. The day was flawless—the twins playing in the snow, the tree ready for transport, a hot drink ready to warm her insides from head to toes. Why then did she feel as if she might cry any moment?

Luke set the basket of food on the tailgate and produced sandwiches and plump, juicy pears before pouring steaming mugs of hot chocolate for both of them.

Leaning against the truck and sipping his drink, he wore a contented expression as he watched the kids play. Kiley blinked away tears, memorizing the moment to relive later.

"Here, try this. See what you think." Lazily, Luke picked up the plate of sandwiches offering them to her.

Almost belligerently she took one, biting into the thick bread and meat, wishing she could sink her teeth into Luke instead.

"What is this? Chicken?" A not quite familiar flavor burst across her tongue. It was delicious.

Luke grinned and shook his head. "Smoked pheasant. Tastes a little like chicken. According to my research, in

England they're called partridges."

Finishing her sandwich, Kate hesitated as she reached for a pear. The word partridge teased her brain. "Hey, you're serving the food in the song."

"You said you loved that song the last time we heard it together."

She felt a blush rush upward and knew her cheeks were red from more than the cold. The last time she'd heard that song they'd had great sex in his truck—again.

"We've got a pear, a tree and a partridge." He laughed self-consciously. "I had to improvise."

"Why?"

"I want to be your true love, Kiley. I want to give you the world." Luke stepped closer, tipping her chin so she had to meet his gaze as he quoted the words.

"On the first day of Christmas my true love gave to me—a partridge in a pear tree." After his voice turned husky from emotion, he paused and cleared his throat before continuing.

"I said I'd never marry again, and maybe I won't." He touched his thumb to her mouth, stroking it against the seam of her lips. "It depends on what you say."

"Exactly what are you offering?" Anticipation hummed through her, warming her from her toes to her flushed cheeks.

"I want to live together, watch the kids grow up together, snuggle in bed together, and make love whenever we want." He cupped her face between his big hands and said the words she needed to hear. "I love you, Kiley. Will you marry me?"

Stunned by his unexpected proposal, she wrapped her arms around his neck, hiding her face against his coat while she composed herself.

"Well now, I didn't mean to scare you to death, sweet-heart. If it's something you don't want to consider—"

"Oh my God, Luke," Kiley looked up and interrupted, poking him in the chest. "I love you so much. I don't even know how it happened. You just crept up on me."

She paused, staring at the kids instead of him, and then said more sedately, "I love you too."

"So that's a yes?" he asked gruffly.

"That's a definite yes," she murmured, brushing her lips across his.

"We need to buy a puppy. Then you'll have everything you once said you wanted."

"What's that?" he asked with a quizzical look.

"A dog, a patch of ground, and two point five kids," she gazed up at him, watching his dear face crinkle in a smile when her words finally sank in.

Epilogue

L UKE SMILED AS he surveyed the stretch of cars going all the way back to the main road. The website had worked better than expected.

He'd made enough money off his trees last winter to plant more and to put in a vegetable patch in the spring.

His plantings had also included a field of pumpkins because his research indicated that they were big sellers in the fall. Today's crowd proved that to be true. Dads and moms tried to keep up with their kids as they raced through the open field, inspecting the different varieties before choosing the perfect one.

Kiley had even taken a pumpkin carving class and Danvers Farm now offered "Let's Make a Jack-O-Lantern" sessions. Kiley had put the sign-up sheet right on the checkout counter. Business was brisk. And that wasn't all.

After he'd attended a farm auction and snagged an old hay wagon and harness dirt cheap, he and Kiley had spent a good part of the summer learning how to manage horses hooked to a wagon carrying people.

It had been crazy fun and more than a few times they'd used *practice* as an excuse to meet up for a quickie in the back field.

Kiley said they needed to keep their taboo trysts because with kids to contend with, fucking was cheaper therapy than a shrink. The woman had an ornery streak in her a mile wide. He loved it. He loved her.

The kids got so they just snickered and rolled their eyes when the mention of horses and hay wagons came up.

But mixed in with shenanigans in the wagon bed, Luke and Kiley had actually learned to handle the team. They'd added it to the website in their menu of fun, and the reservations poured in.

They'd been doing hayrides every weekend for a month. And they never had an unfilled spot in a wagon.

Doug had pulled together a group of volunteers who built Marcie's Farm Palisade. Hay tunnels, slides, and a climbing wall offered more kid fun for the farm tours that were booked all the way to the end of next month.

Jeannie, Luke's mother-in-law had gotten into the spirit of things and set up a concession stand for another source of revenue coming in. That had turned into three food carts and two additional local women to run them.

After the holidays, when things settled down, he planned to take Kiley, the twins, and the new baby to Austin. He wanted to visit Angel House first. It seemed important to him that she see where he'd been before he met her.

While they were in Texas, she'd also meet the rest of the men he'd served with. But most of all, if he admitted it, he wanted to show off Kiley Endicott Danvers, and the family she'd given him.

He sighed and slung his arm around her shoulders, pulling her close as they walked toward the barn.

"You fine, secret agent man?" she teased, stopping a moment to study his face.

He gazed back, taking in her big smile and the glow of happiness in her eyes.

"Sweetheart," he answered gruffly. "With you by my side, I'm better than fine."

The End

Smoke, Inc.
Stand-Alone, Shared-World, Titles

The stories in this series are loosely related and can be read in any order. Don't be surprised if you discover your favorite main character, cast in a supporting role in a later Smoke Inc. adventure.

Each couple pursue their *happy-ever-after* from their first sizzling kiss to the end.

<u>Smoke Inc. Titles</u>
Taboo Frequency
Cowboy Burn
PHATT Farm
Rhythm
EAZY Loving, PHATT Farm Too

About author, Gem Sivad

Hi. Nice to meet you. Having finished this book, you know I write about people who fall in love and commit to spending a lifetime together.

I've discovered that genre doesn't matter. Whether I'm writing about the Old West, witches and shifters, or a Christmas tree farmer and a widow in lust, passion seems to shine its light, pointing toward love.

Although I have hermit tendencies, occasionally I come out of the writer's den to meet readers at book signing events. Hope to see you there. But in case we miss each other, you can find me at the cyber locations below.

Website:
GemSivad.com

BookBub:
bookbub.com/profile/gem-sivad

Goodreads:
goodreads.com/author/show/3154528.Gem_Sivad

FaceBook:
facebook.com/GemSivadAuthor

Twitter:
twitter.com/gemsivad

Sign up for
GemSivad.com/Dreamcatcher